Second City Trilogy

IRISHTOWN PRESS

Cónal Creedon is a playwright, novelist and documentary filmmaker.

www.conalcreedon.com

Second City Trilogy

CÓNAL CREEDON

IRISHTOWN PRESS

BLOOD IN THE ALLEY – IRISHTOWN PRODUCTIONS PRESENTS

AFTER LUKE &
WHEN I WAS GOD

SMASH-HIT OF NEW YORK THEATRE FESTIVAL 2009

SENSATION AT SHANGHAI WORLD EXPO 2010 – CHINA

BY CÓNAL CREEDON   DIRECTED BY GEOFF GOULD.
STARRING: DONNCHA CROWLEY, DENIS FOLEY, AIDAN O'HARE

CORK ARTS THEATRE
TUESDAY 13TH JULY TO SATURDAY 31ST OF JULY
SHOW STARTS: 8PM   TICKET PRICE: €18 • STRICTLY OVER 16s
BOOKING: 0214505624 10-5PM (AFTER 2PM SAT'S.) NO PERFORMANCES ON SUNDAYS.

 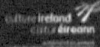

Acclaim and Reviews

As written by Cónal Creedon, such moments resound with wince-inducing authenticity before they are eclipsed by an inspirational twist — words, inflected with the faintly Scandinavian accent of Munster, soar like a bracing breeze off the River Lee.
NEW YORK TIMES, 2013. Andy Webster.

Fathers and sons and the damage done: this is the theme, with variations, of the Cork writer Cónal Creedon's fine plays "After Luke" and "When I Was God," which can be seen in a nearly pitch-perfect production. Mr Creedon's words are enough to create a world that is at once comic and dramatic, poetic and musical.
NEW YORK TIMES, 2009. Rachel Saltz.

I don't know why Cónal Creedon hasn't been produced on Broadway yet. Certainly his plays are as deserving as any recent work from Ireland that has made that cut. In fact, he has more to say, more concisely, than just about any of his dramatic contemporaries.
IRISH CENTRAL – NEW YORK. 2013. Cahir O'Doherty.

Irish playwrights (from Yeats and Wilde and Synge and Shaw on down to now) are always good going on great, and the latest in that endless chain is the all but unknown in America, Cónal Creedon. Unknown no longer, Creedon's short, idiosyncratic "After Luke," and even shorter, punchier "When I Was God," comprise a disturbing two-hour double-bill. Idiosyncratic? Bite off any hunk of either work; it's all as chewy as leather yet weirdly digestible. None of this would be unfamiliar to, let's say, D.H. Lawrence, or, for that matter, George Orwell. What hasn't been heard before is the thorny voice of 48-year-old Cónal Creedon of County Cork, Ireland, who, from all reports, is

a lot gentler in the flesh than on paper.
NEW YORK VILLAGER, 2009. Jerry Tallmer.

Creedon's rootedness in Cork qualifies him to chronicle the transformations that not just Cork City, but all of Ireland, caused by the economic boom of the 1990s – called the Celtic Tiger – and the aftermath

At times it feels Beckett-like, you might think the people are too unusual to exist but they actually do.
NEW YORK CITY ARTS, 2009. Gwen Orel.

I imagine there are few things harder to be than a contemporary Irish playwright. Given the theatrical history of the Emerald Isle, its lyric tradition, it must be either a very daring or very foolish individual indeed who steps up to be measured against the likes of the Irish literary pantheon. On the daring end falls Cónal Creedon, author of After Luke and When I Was God. The two plays are the latter parts of Creedon's seriocomic Second City Trilogy, focusing on life in present-day County Cork. Both plays are about the family dynamic, specifically the relationships between fathers and sons. In After Luke, two half-brothers, Maneen and Son, share a memory so terrible that it sets them at odds with each other all their lives. In the center is Dadda, Maneen's father, who does his best to keep the peace but can only do so much. As he sagely says "… when two elephants go to war, 'tis the grass gets trampled."

In When I Was God, Dino lives in the shadow of his father's regrets, and under the pressure of his expectations. It's a classic plot, the father using the son to live the life he wished he could have had. To tell the rest would rob the reader of one of the funniest moments of the evening. Creedon's main device in these pieces is repetition. I found myself laughing uproariously as the words stayed the same but the meaning was in constant shift, each repetition raising the stakes to a beautifully bittersweet conclusion – driving the action and the comedy. Creedon's show holds up very well against the pantheon of Irish theatre, taking chances with some very risky devices. It's a fun

night out, and I'd be interested to see the trilogy in its entirety; if the first act is as entertaining as the last two, it would be well worth it.
NY THEATER REVIEW – Peter Schuyler, August 5, 2009

The highlight of last year's theatre in Shanghai came all the way from Cork in Irish playwright's Cónal Creedon's double-header of short plays — powerful, yet punctuated with humour, lyrical and richly colloquial. They were terrific!
THAT'S SHANGHAI MAGAZINE [China], March 2011.

This is contemporary theatre that plays like the works of a past master. The work of Irish playwright Cónal Creedon, are quite simply a delight, [but] not in an all sunshine and light way. On a sparse stage on which the characters can only live or die, it lives. Underlying all is a love of language and a keen observance of detail — Creedon is lyrical, and uses rhyme and rhythm, without being showy, and enriches with the Cork colloquial without alienating — Come back soon, you are always welcome on the Shanghai stage.
TALK SHANGHAI. China. Arts Editor.

They were discussing what should go into the Irish Millennium Time-Capsule. If they are looking for something to represent Ireland, how about Cónal Creedon's *Under the Goldie Fish?* It's so off the wall, that it shouldn't ring true, but the most frightening fact is that it does …
THE SUNDAY INDEPENDENT, 2008. Eilís O'Hanlon.

The Cure is a dramatic creation that straddles what we once were and what we have become. It examines closely the fracture at the heart of our contemporary experience — scavenging the thesaurus for sufficient superlatives for this fine piece of writing — yes we liked it. We liked it a lot.
THE IRISH EXAMINER, 2005. Ian Kilroy.

Everyone loves the Irish. It's just a fact. Creedon's script is a rich fusion of melancholy poetry and affable banter. Aidan O'Hare and 'The Cure' are a match made in monologue heaven. Its potency lies in the profound ability of the playwright and the actor to connect directly with people. 'The Cure' is a truly fine piece of theatre, one that is Irish to its core but anything but provincial in its scope. You couldn't ask for anything more than this.
SMART SHANGHAI MAGAZINE, March 2011.

A one-man show at the Ke Centre proves that you don't need a huge cast to produce a hit — their recent collaboration with Irishtown Productions proves that they are on top of their game. Cork playwright Cónal Creedon's gritty soliloquy 'The Cure' saw Irish actor Aidan O'Hare command the stage as a man left behind by a racing economy and changing city. Creedon's use of language is dizzyingly attractive. He manipulates repetition to great effect, bringing the opening lines back several times in chilling sonata form. As for the staging, the Ke Centre's stark space was the perfect backdrop for a bleak but redemptive piece of drama.
ASIA CITY NETWORK, Shanghai, China, 2011.

A pair of tenderly drawn plays by Cónal Creedon, set in Creedon's native Cork, probe the tough love and tough hurt — exchanged by men in Irish Families. Both plays — are intimately conceived and performed, tracing in chiaroscuro, the intersection between kinship and machismo.
NEW YORKER MAGAZINE.

The Cure is the bittersweet tale of a man who has emotionally lost his way. As with the previous two plays, Creedon explores the frustrations of average lives, to the backdrop of historical happenings in the playwright's hometown. And as with the previous two, the script is lyrical and rich with colloquialism, the melancholy lifted with moments of delightful amusement. ("When the chemistry goes in a relationship, he reflects on marriage and drink, "There's nothing for it

but to take more chemicals – A fine piece of theatre …
THAT'S SHANGHAI MAGAZINE, Urbanatomy Shanghai, March 2011.

A complex enthralling piece of theatre that boasts the dual achievement of entertaining and educating — a testament to Creedon's shrewd writing skill.
THE IRISH INDEPENDENT, 2005.

Vigorously sustained by stylish performances and an ingenious script, which marries comedy and pathos with a sure hand. They'll love it. It's impossible not to.
THE IRISH TIMES, 2001.

Cónal Creedon's Second City Trilogy is a significant dramatic achievement. Creedon constructs predicaments for his characters that ring true universally. In three companion pieces that play logically together, the playwright puts a marginal view of society centre-stage, and, with warmth and humour, offers a view of life from the side-lines. What ensues is a solid replaying of a classic and timeless family conflict. Taken altogether, the Second City Trilogy is an important a landmark in drama, its achievement is to find a theatrical language that can accommodate the poor and depressed Ireland that we have come from, and the new, confusing, complex reality we now find ourselves in. Creedon, director Geoff Gould, and the cast deserve credit not only for offering up an entertaining night of theatre, but for contributing to our understanding of where we have come from and where we are going. Any drama that can do both is indeed worthy of praise.
THE IRISH EXAMINER. 2005. Ian Kilroy.

I got to see the Cure at the half moon theatre last night. It is terrific. It's great fun. It's just fantastic. Just so well done by Mikel Murfi. It's a credit to Cónal Creedon. Don't miss this play, you need to go and see it - the cultural highlight of Cork2005.
OPINION LINE, 96fm.

Creedon's great gift seems to be observation, 45 tense, funny and pointed minutes, convincing and memorably skilful. When I Was God, is both a treat and a treasure.
THE IRISH TIMES.

This play operated on two levels, it was hilarious but poignant. Creedon's gift is his ability to distil the very essence of his environment. It is this sense of place and people and his gently anarchic view of life which makes his works so deliciously attractive.
THE IRISH EXAMINER.

Creedon's play shifts easily between the past and the present, revealing a sharp ear for dialogue, keen eye for observation and a deep affection for his characters as Creedon brings a deft pathos and humour to the tragicomedy of a peculiar father son relationship, a delight that demands to be savoured.
THE SUNDAY TRIBUNE.

Second City Trilogy

CÓNAL CREEDON

IRISHTOWN PRESS

Published in 2018 by Irishtown Press

Irishtownpress@gmail.com

© Cónal Creedon 2019

The moral right of the author has been asserted. A catalogue record for this book is available from the British Library.

ISBN 978–0–9557644–8–6

Book design by John Foley. www.bitedesign.com

Original cover artwork by Eileen Healy – permanent collection of Crawford Gallery, Cork.

Second City Trilogy was produced with assistance from Arts Office Cork City Council, Arts Council of Ireland, Culture Ireland and Cork 2005 European Capital of Culture.

This book is dedicated to:
Michael Delaney – who gave my fingers a hand.
Ellen Fayer – who managed to keep the show on the road.
Róisín McAvinney – who put the ball in the net.

With special gratitude to so many people who helped to bring the trilogy from page to stage: Fiona O'Toole, John Foley and Lisa Sheridan – Bite Design, Pat Kiernan, Steve Manning, Michael Lonergan, Martin Lynch, Nancy Hawkes, Valarie Byrne, Mary McCarthy, Thomas McCarthy, Geoff Gould, Gerry Barnes, Michael Mellamphy, Tim Ruddy, Rosita Janbakhsh, Hua Peihua, Ciarán O'Reilly, Charlotte Moore, Pat Ledwidge, Liz Meany, Christine Sisk – Culture Ireland, Shanghai Writers' Association, Red Kettle Theatre Company, Opera House – Cork, Irish Repertory Theatre – New York, Shanghai Repertory Theatre – Shanghai.

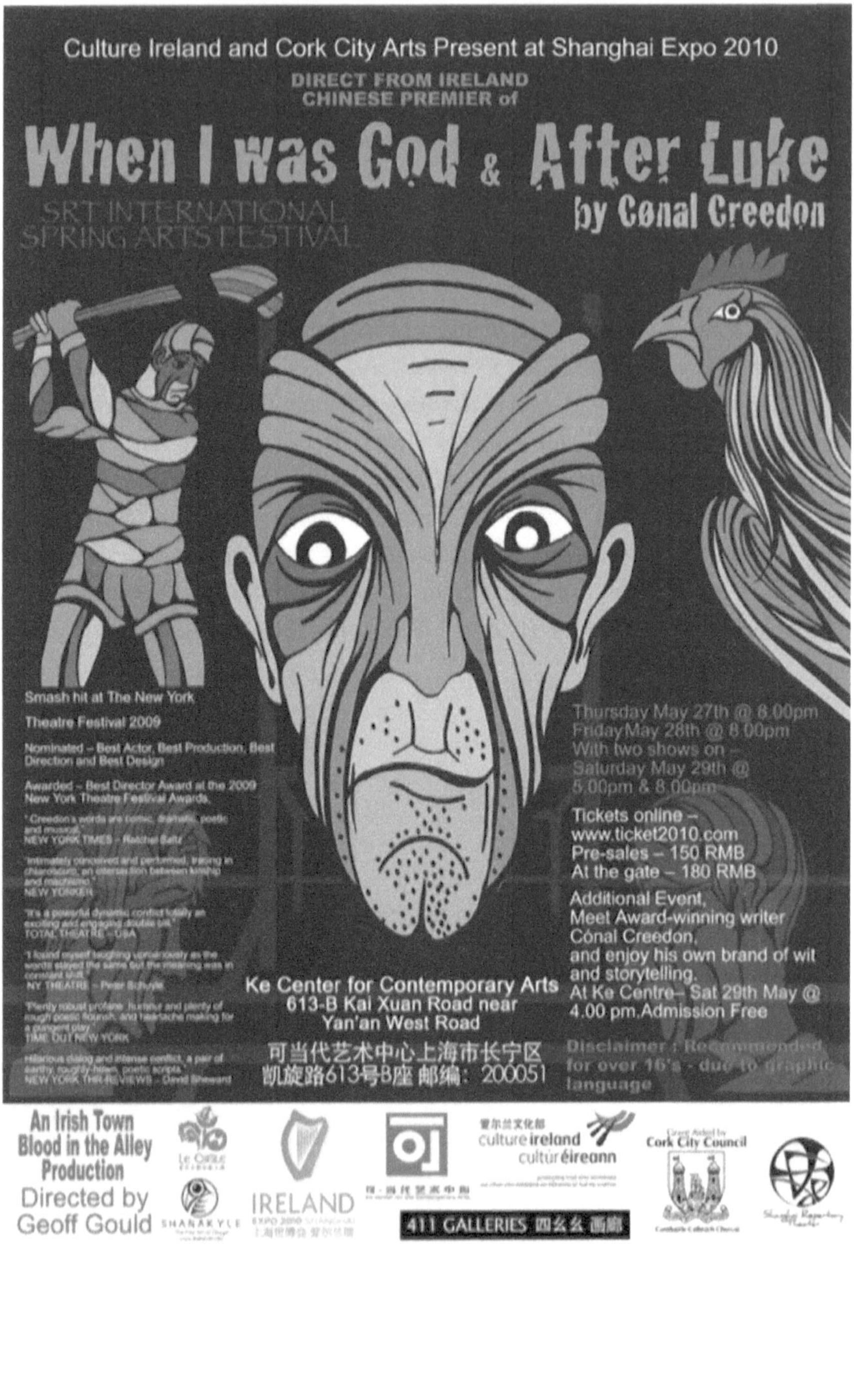

Culture Ireland and Cork City Arts Present at Shanghai Expo 2010
DIRECT FROM IRELAND
CHINESE PREMIER of
When I was God & After Luke
by Conal Creedon
SRT INTERNATIONAL
SPRING ARTS FESTIVAL
Smash hit at The New York
Theatre Festival 2009
Nominated – Best Actor, Best Production, Best Direction and Best Design
Awarded – Best Director Award at the 2009 New York Theatre Festival Awards.
NEW YORK TIMES – Rachel Saltz
NEW YORKER
TOTAL THEATRE – USA
NY THEATRE – Peter Schuyler
TIME OUT NEW YORK
Thursday May 27th @ 8.00pm
FridayMay 28th @ 8.00pm
With two shows on –
Saturday May 29th @
5.00pm & 8.00pm
Tickets online –
www.ticket2010.com
Pre-sales – 150 RMB
At the gate – 180 RMB
Additional Event,
Meet Award-winning writer
Cónal Creedon,
and enjoy his own brand of wit and storytelling.
At Ke Centre– Sat 29th May @ 4.00 pm.Admission Free
Ke Center for Contemporary Arts
613-B Kai Xuan Road near
Yan'an West Road
可当代艺术中心上海市长宁区
凯旋路613号B座 邮编: 200051
Disclaimer : Recommended for over 16's - due to graphic language
An Irish Town
Blood in the Alley
Production
Directed by
Geoff Gould
SHANAKYLE
IRELAND
EXPO 2010
culture ireland
cultúr éireann
Cork City Council
411 GALLERIES

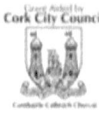

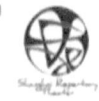

CONTENTS

FOREWORD

Cónal Creedon is acutely aware that there's no room for ironic gestures at a penalty shootout. It is difficult to make art from sport, although there is much art in sport itself: ask anyone who's been to a recent Munster Hurling Final. In order to make art-art or theatre-art a great deal of meditation and distancing has to occur in the mind of the playwright. When the crowd roared in the Shed at Turner's Cross it was not done to salute a dramatic monologue, but to acknowledge a split second response, a bend of the ball, a billowing of the net. What Cónal Creedon has succeeded in doing in this Second City Trilogy is unique, uniquely Cónal and uniquely Cork. As dramatist he has become both the referee and the player. But sport is only one part of it: each of the lives portrayed here is at once desolate and hilarious. That's Creedon's great gift to the audience.

Who can forget the sublime and deeply emotional experience of these plays from that long and busy summer of *Cork2005*? Frankie McCaffrey and Donncha Crowley's haunted seriousness, and Denis Foley's brilliance and, earlier, Mikel Murfi's complete mastery and possession of 'The Cure' followed by Michael Patric's hugely charged repossession of the Cork past.

> *'But then, just for a whiff of a second subtle scent of sherbet,*
> *drifting down from Linehan's Sweet Factory,*
> *would carry him past the putrid pelts of the tannery,*
> *and on to the first taste of human waste at Poulraddy.*
>
> *Turnin' right onto Leitrim Street and there'd be no mistaking*
> *the warmth of the moist malt of brewing stout –*
> *billowing from Murphy's stack.'*

It was not just the writing but the timing, the marvellous directing of Geoff Gould and Gerry Barnes' creation of a resonating context in the Half Moon Theatre.

'Do ya know what I did I'll tell ya what I did.'

'I think of the pleasure that these plays gave at an important moment in the cultural life of the Republic's second city. Those were days when I felt worn down by the necessities of a lugubrious arts structure: I can't believe that these plays once existed inside a Cultural Capital file called *Project Execution Plan*. They remind me of what I always intuited: arts organisations are temporary things, but art is permanent. When 'Dadda,' 'Son' and 'Maneen' create a choral work of theatre together in *After Luke* time itself is defeated, bureaucracy is,

'Like I'm squeezed out.
Squeezed out by the golden boy.'

The atmosphere in the Half Moon Theatre was electric; something special was happening in theatre in 2005 and everyone in the audience knew it. Here was a player who togged out week after week and was finally allowed to take the penalties in the ultimate theatre, the Half Moon.

'And if there's one thing I've learned over the years:
When the chemistry goes in a relationship –
there's only one thing for it.
Take more chemicals!'

In each of these plays there are wanderers, not just ramblers through the flat of the city, but wanderers morally and socially. There are sins of the fathers visited upon sons; there is exile and property, the impossibility of one and the emptiness of the latter. The material of these plays, I mean the personal mythologies behind them, had previous incarnations in prose fiction and on radio. *After Luke* was originally commissioned by the Church of Ireland and performed on RTÉ and Creedon's collection of stories, *Pancho and Lefty Ride Out*, was published by the Collins Press in 1995. But the combination of the Cork Opera House, Blood in the Alley Theatre and the European Capital of Culture led to a new set of possibilities for the unique tone and tension of the material. At the time we had many interesting discussions about this material, many phone calls and meetings on the streets that have acquired a Cavafy-like mythical life, that Creedon matrix of Coburg, Leitrim and Devonshire streets. And in a time full of exhaustion I know that the spirits of my colleagues in *Cork2005*, Mary McCarthy and Tony Sheehan, were lifted by encounters with these scripts. They were pure art and nothing else. Now they belong to the theatre, permanently. Even before they were performed they had the feel of permanence.

The theatre of Cónal Creedon, then, is both a cure and a miracle. We take our seats as prodigal sons, hoping to escape from the mind-set of life's referee yet knowing that winning is everything: 'I've never known a man to give up his Harty Cup medal – never! They'll carry it with them to the grave' as Father says in *When I Was God*. It is no wonder that this Trilogy ran for over three months at the Half Moon Theatre and later transferred to the main stage of the Cork Opera House. In the years to come I hope that many others, searching for meaning, searching for a lyrical, Lorca-like theatre, those walking for a cure, will join the twelve thousand lucky ones who sat enthralled by Cónal Creedon in the year 2005.

Thomas McCarthy
Deputy Director Cork 2005.
European Capital Of Culture.
Director of Programme.

1ST IRISH 2008

A THREE WEEK FESTIVAL
OF IRISH THEATRE
ACROSS NEW YORK
www.1stIrish.org

CONOR McPHERSON
ENDA WALSH
URSULA RANI SARMA
MORNA REGAN
PAT KINEVANE
FIONA WALSH
OWEN McCAFFERTY
CONAL CREEDON
LIAM HEYLIN OSCAR WILDE

ABBIE SPALLEN

GARY DUGGAN

DANIEL REARDON

THE PLAYERS THEATRE
ORIGIN THEATRE COMPANY
NYU GLUCKSMAN IRELAND HOUSE

KEEGAN THEATRE COMPANY
59E59 THEATERS
MANHATTAN THEATRE SOURCE

SEPTEMBER 6 TO 28
THE AMERICAN IRISH HISTORICAL SOCIETY   59E59 THEATERS

Second City Trilogy

The Cure, When I Was God & After Luke

Awarded
**Best
Director**

1st Irish New York Theatre Awards.
New York. 2009

Nominated
**Best
Production**

1st Irish New York Theatre Awards.
New York. 2009

Awarded
**Best
Actor**

1st Irish New York Theatre Awards.
New York. 2013

Nominated
**Best
Playwright**

1st Irish New York
Theatre Awards. New York 2013

Awarded
**Best
Actor**

ICA Wicklow Federation
Drama Festival. 2014

Awarded
**Best
Supporting
Actor**

ICA Wicklow Federation
Drama Festival. 2014

SECOND CITY TRILOGY

Commissioned by European Capital of Culture

SECOND CITY TRILOGY. Three stage plays [The Cure, When I Was God & After Luke] – conceived as a tragicomic exploration of various father-son relationships, set against the social, historical and topographical background of Cork City, the second city of the Republic of Ireland. The trilogy is comprised of three short plays and is structured such that the casting requirements of all three plays can be met by three actors, with each actor appearing in two of the plays. THE CURE. In times of personal crisis, either a cure or a miracle may be required to turn a life around. Our anti-hero is incapable of confronting and dealing with a number of personal issues. It is a recurring theme in his life, a theme that has been handed down, from generation to generation through the male line in his family, like a baton in a relay race. We meet him trawling the streets looking for an early morning pub in search of a cure. But fate takes a hand to his feet and the streets of Cork become his road to Damascus.

WHEN I WAS GOD. It's FAI Cup Final day. Referee Dino Keegan is retiring from the game. At half-time the spotlight of self-doubt shines directly down on Dino as the ghosts of his past visit him in his dressing room. On the field of dreams the referee is God, but what happens when God is made man?

AFTER LUKE. Is inspired by the parable of the Prodigal Son, in St. Luke's Gospel. It explores greed-driven frenzy surrounding the property market at the height of the Celtic Tiger economy. The action unfolds in that contentious place where concrete and asphalt meet pasture and stone and urban necessity collides with the rural idyll - with devastatingly tragic consequences.

PRODUCTION DETAILS

Irish Premiere

27th June 2005. The Half Moon Theatre, Cork Opera House. Cork.
Ireland.
Cork Opera House/Blood in The Alley Production.

Cast* .... DONNCHA CROWLEY (*When I Was God, After Luke*)
.... FRANKIE MCCAFFERTY (*When I Was God, After Luke*)
.... MICHAEL PATRIC (*After Luke, The Cure*)
Director...GEOFF GOULD
Set Design ....PAT MURRAY
Lighting Design...LIZZIE POWELL
Sound Design.. SIMON MCHALE
Stage Manager .... ELLEN FAYER
Production Manager...................................... MARIA YOUNG

*Mikel Murfi performed *The Cure* as a solo piece in March 2005.
Denis Foley (2nd Cast) performed *When I Was God* & *After Luke*.

American Premiere – (*When I Was God*)

September 8th 2008. Manhattan Theatre Source. New York. USA.
Plays Upstairs, New York Production.

Cast... MICHAEL MELLAMPHY
.... GARY GREGG
Director.. TIM RUDDY

AMERICAN PREMIERE – (*After Luke/ When I Was God*)

July 29th 2009. Irish Repertory Theatre. New York. USA.
Irish Repertory Theatre, New York Production.

Cast........... MICHAEL MELLAMPHY (*When I Was God, After Luke*)
.... GARY GREGG (*When I Was God, After Luke*)
....COLIN LANE (*After Luke*)
Director... TIM RUDDY
Set Design .... LEX LIANG
Lighting Design.. BRIAN NASON
Sound Design ....SHANNON SLATTON
Production Manager ....APRIL A KLINE
Stage Manager .... JANICE M BRANDINE

AMERICAN PREMIERE – (*The Cure*)

September 8th 2013. Ryan's Daughter Theatre. New York. USA.
Green Room Theatre Production.

Cast.. MICHAEL MELLAMPHY
Director... TIM RUDDY

CHINESE PREMIERE – (*After Luke / When I Was God*)

May 27th 2010. Ke Centre for Performing Arts, Shanghai. China.
Culture Ireland Programme at World Expo Shanghai 2010.
Irishtown / Blood In The Alley / Shanghai Repertory Theatre
Company Production.

Cast.............. DONNCHA CROWLEY (*After Luke, When I Was God*)
.... DENIS FOLEY (*After Luke, When I Was God*)
.... AIDAN O'HARE [*After Luke*)
Director.. GEOFF GOULD
Sound Design .... NIALL TONER
Lighting Design.. ELIZABETH POWELL
Costume Design... LIV MONAGHAN
Stage Manager .... MICHAEL LONERGAN
Production Manager .... JESSICA FINKEN

CHINESE PREMIERE – (*The Cure*)

March 16th 2011. Ke Centre for Performing Arts, Shanghai. China.
Irishtown Productions / Shanghai Repertory Theatre Company
Production.

Cast.. AIDAN O'HARE
Director.. CÓNAL CREEDON
Lighting... MICHAEL LONERGAN
Production Manager .... STEVE MANNING
Sound Design .... ANTH KALEY

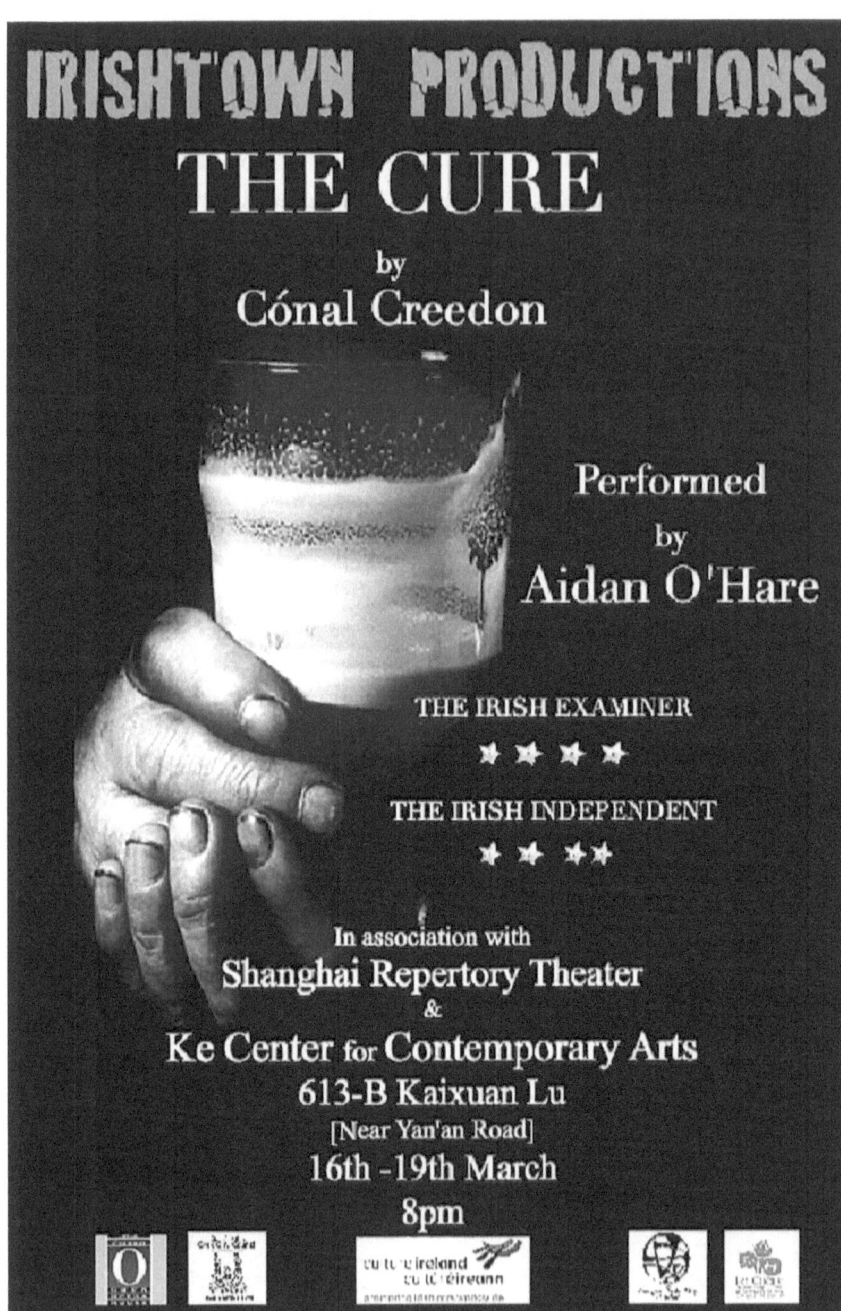

IRISHTOWN PRODUCTIONS
THE CURE

by
Cónal Creedon

Performed
by
Aidan O'Hare

THE IRISH EXAMINER
✦ ✦ ✦

THE IRISH INDEPENDENT
✦ ✦ ✦✦

In association with
Shanghai Repertory Theater
&
Ke Center for Contemporary Arts
613-B Kaixuan Lu
[Near Yan'an Road]
16th –19th March
8pm

THE CURE

BY

CÓNAL CREEDON

THE CURE

by Cónal Creedon

Of the three plays that make up *The Second City Trilogy* – THE CURE is the most rooted in the history and topography of Cork City. The play presents both a physical and an emotional journey through history. There is a sense that the audience is brought on a walking tour through time, where street names, landmarks, industries, individual shopkeepers and traders all seem to blend seamlessly with unfolding events, past and present.

Set against three of the most cataclysmic events in the recent history of Cork City,

- – The burning of Cork by the Black and Tans in the 1920s.
- – The closure of Dunlop and Ford motor works and the deep recession of the 1980s.
- – The boom of the Celtic Tiger economy in the 2000s.

THE CURE was written in 2005 – at the height of the Celtic Tiger economic boom. The play examines the effect of poverty during a boom time – that feeling of being left behind. The Cure explores three generations of a family – grandfather, father and son – each unable to cope with issues in their personal lives, choose to redirect and blame the consequences of their own failings, by projecting onto the greater issues of the time in which they live. It is a recurring theme that has been handed down from generation to generation – grandfather to father to son, like a baton in a relay race.

At times of personal crisis, either a cure or a miracle may be required to turn a life around. Having lived through the recession of the 1980s, our narrator now finds himself caught in the slipstream of the booming Celtic Tiger economy and is unable to confront a number of issues in his personal life. It's Christmas week, we meet him trawling the streets of Cork looking for an early morning pub in search of a cure. But fate takes a hand to his feet and the streets of Cork become his road to Damascus.

THE CURE

CAST: One male, early 40s – to play multiple roles.

Note:

The NARRATOR is in his early 40s. He appears to be a bit the worse for wear. He is not drunk, more distracted and deluded, suffering the ill effects of having been on a drinking spree for a number of days. The logic and emotion of the play is explored through the thin veil of guilt-fuelled morality and self-justification an alcoholic can experience while waiting for pub opening time and a cure.

Costume Suggestion – a long navy or black overcoat. The shadow cast while in the classroom scene will give the impression of a clerical soutane

Text Notes:

For the most part the play is an internal monologue expressed verbally – but periodically the internal words become spoken dialog with the Narrator playing the various characters.

Tech Notes:

Soundscape Notes [SFX]:

For the most part the soundscape will involve various musical links.

The overall sound motif will comprise a number of variations of the traditional christmas carol – 'In The Bleak Midwinter'. Each variation should identify the required atmosphere.

Example: Trumpet solo could be used at opening of play. A slightly out of tune brass band [Salvation Army type] could be used during the street scene. Hand held bells version could be used for the scene in the church.

Other Music:
Karaoke – backing track – Jennifer Rush, 'The Power Of Love'.
Grand Finale – maybe a powerful brass band version of 'Going Home'.

Lighting Notes [LX]:
Lighting should be cold and stark – maybe three dominant colours – red, blue and white. The overall effect should be isolation of the character – do not fill the stage with light – but rather isolate and identify certain locations and moods with pools of light.

A very strong red lit backdrop at opening and final tableau onto which we project the silhouette of NARRATOR as he enters & exits the stage. The opening and closing tableau lighting should be visually similar, because the words at beginning and end of play mirror each other – yet are expressed with different meaning and interpretation.

A specific church rose window gobo when NARRATOR is in the church scene. Various combinations of red & blue for the church scene to present an undefined stained glass effect.

The flashback scenes with the Christian Brother [BROTHER KEENAN] and the Karaoke scenes should be significantly different from the rest of the play. Each one a set piece of specific sound and lighting to create a sense of heightened realism.

[Each time BROTHER KEENAN materialises as a memory flashback in the classroom scenes – a very specific LX effect is required. It should be snap action, clear and defined. Such as a large stark skewed gobo of sixteen pane old-style classroom window projected on backdrop. BROTHER KEENAN should be under lit by birdie lamp, such that it will project a gigantic clean shadow of BROTHER KEENAN on the backdrop.

His hand actions and gestures on stage will be exaggerated by the projection of his shadow – presenting a sense of a giant man bearing down on a small boy.

The Karaoke Club scene should also be very defined and specific – snap into action with a specific mirror-ball effect.

I

Opening SFX: Tune: Bleak Mid Winter.
Trumpet solo – organic not computer generated – slightly imperfect –
sense of Salvation Army – lonesome.

Opening LX: NARRATOR slowly arrives on stage in silhouette, to
strong red glow on backdrop. As the trumpet solo comes to an end the
NARRATOR should be centre stage on his mark – for snap light change
from red back drop silhouette to stark white spot light.

NARRATOR:
>A sleepy Saturday mornin' on Half Moon Street
>and just around the corner?
>Christmas.
>
>I'm walkin' off a bit of self-inflicted pain, you know how it is
>…
>Three days on the ran-tan.
>Three whole days – drinkin' me seasonal bonus.
>You know how it is – when the belly's had a skin-full,
>the mind is willing – but the body isn't able.
>Well, that's how it is.
>
>Just out for a scove – meself on me own,
>no particular place to go. [*gesture to Chuck Berry*]
>Just …
>Just followin' me nose …
>
>[*Pause as previous line conjures up a memory – he is amused by*
>*the memory*]
>
>Just follow yer nose?
>That's what me Grandda used to do.

A great man for followin' his nose was me Grandda.
On me mother's soul – he could find his way to work –
blindfolded.

All the way from his front door step up on Dublin Hill,
down into the belly of the city – just …
Just followin' his nose …

II

The first thing that would hit my Grandda and he leaving the house
would be the thick country smell of cattle,
from the dealers fields beyond the grotto in Blackpool.

Led on like a …
Like a bull by the ring,
he'd close his eyes and follow his nose.

Past the stale stench of last night's stout and cigarette smoke
from the string of pubs along Dublin Street.
Past the Glen Hall – the full length of Thomas Davis Street.

And with the first hint of crusty bread coming from the ovens
of Cuthbert's Bakery over on Great William O'Brien Street,
he'd know he was at Blackpool Church.

Then that sweet smell of molten sugar –
The shawlies making toffee apples up on Gerald Griffin Street,
would carry him past the oak casks of the distillery
and onto the Watercourse Road.

[Deep inhale through nose]

Ahhh pleasure …

A pleasure – cut short by the piercing, deathly, toxic,
foul cloud coming from the slaughterhouse off Denny's Lane.

But then, just for a whiff of a second the subtle scent of
sherbet,
drifting down from Linehan's Sweet Factory,
would carry him past the putrid pelts of the tannery,
and on to the first taste of human waste at Poulraddy.

Turnin' right onto Leitrim Street and there'd be no mistaking
the warmth of the moist malt of brewing stout –
billowing from Murphy's Stack.
He knew then he was on the right track.
So, he'd put the hands into the pockets – and whistle …

Whistle all the way from Poulraddy Harbour,
to the Home Farm Stores.
Eyes wide shut.

And though still out of sight – at the corner of Pine Street,
the River Lee and Carroll's Quay would come into scent.
[sniff] Low at high tide.
[sniff – react to bad smell] High at low tide.

Wouldn't turn left nor right,
but keep on straight to Three Points Corner –
where Devonshire Street, Leitrim Street and Coburg Street
melt into one.
He'd stay right on track,
being passed from scent to scent like the baton in a relay race.

Spurred on by the aromatic blending of –
Moore's vegetables, Griffin's shoemakers, Noreen's apple tarts,
[sniff] must be Friday 'cause there's kippers in Creedon's,
O'Connell's butchered beef and O'Sullivan's cured bacon.

At Falvey's Corner, he'd stop.
Stop dead.
Struck by a tidal wave of fishy smells from the Baltimore
Stores –
Enough to knock a horse.

And for the first time on his scove,
my Grandda'd open his eyes.
Look back at the eastern face of Shandon.
Where half-past seven means twenty-five to eight.

Then turnin' right onto Bridge Street.

And the fine wines and exotic spices of Madden's,
would carry him 'cross Patrick's Bridge,
through the gateway of the city –
all the way to work –
Just …
Just by following his nose …

[Inhale through nose and sigh]

Ahhh …

III

[brought back to the reality of his situation]

… a sleepy Saturday morning on Half Moon Street,
and just around the corner?
Christmas.

Three days on the ran-tan.
Three whole days drinkin' me seasonal bonus.

You know how it is?
So, I turn into Paul's Street, just walkin' off
a bit of self-inflicted …

Pain? Don't be talkin' to me.
There's a fella standin' outside the Gingerbread
and he strangling a steel guitar – playin' somethin' by
Muddy Waters, or Rory Gallagher, or Joe Dolan, or
somebody?
I dunno …

Too much goin' on in me mind as it is.
Head full of noise.
Seagulls squawking', hawkers hawkin'
and a kango hammer right between me eyes –
drillin' a hole int'v me brain.

And the soles of me shoes pushin' pavement,
like they're tappin' out time.
Tappin' out time 'til the pubs open.
And I'd go back in for the cure.
And by Christ do I need a cure.

But doesn't fate take a hand to me feet,
turn them into French Church Street.
A short cut to the early mornin' pubs on
Fadder Matthew Quay.

Fadder Matthew?
[Ironic dismissive laugh/smile]

He's spinnin' like a top in his grave.
And me?
I'm slinkin' along in the rain,
just punchin' time 'til I can sort the pain.

The pain that's rattlin',
rattlin' 'round in the back a' me …

Brain?! Boiled from drink. Boiled from drink!
But I'm feelin' fine, you know?
Enjoyin' me stroll through the streets.
Just waitin' for the cure.

IV

And that's when I sees him,
in the distance, in black.
That bastard of a man,
the very Reverend – Christian –
Brother Keenan.

His face's out of focus, 'tis the walk I recognise.
And he shuffling along French Church Street – in my
direction.

Trapped! No way out.
My only escape is an about face.
But Christ, I'd lost face to that man once too often in the past.

Jesus!
If the pubs in this town would open at a reasonable hour,
I wouldn't be on this street, at this time, this mornin'
– facin' that bastard!

The things I wouldn't do to that man
if I ever came face to face with him.
Often swore I'd give him a dalk. *[gesture giving a dig]*
Granted now, usually when I be on the jar,
belly full of bravado.

But here I am, on French Church Street, staring him down.
Trapped. Trapped by my own pride.

[Transition: A snap transition from NARRATOR to BROTHER KEENAN.
Note: Transition from NARRATOR to BROTHER KEENAN in classroom to
be sharp, sudden, and clear.
BROTHER KEENAN should present a physical gesture that immediately
informs the audience – This is BROTHER KEENAN.
His voice, gestures and facial expression defined and specific. His facial
expression should be is a painful/cold smile – which can be echoed in the
final scene, but presenting a totally different interpretation.
Costume Suggestion – a long navy or black over coat – the shadow cast
while in the class room will give the impression of a clericals soutane.]

[LX: Lit from beneath BROTHER KEENAN – making him appear to be
more terrifying and also to cast a larger than life sharp shadow of the
Christian Brother upwards onto the background.
Large skewed sixteen pane window gobo projected behind him onto
backdrop – creating impression of a classroom.]

[SFX: BROTHER KEENAN's voice enhanced by reverb – echo of a
classroom effect.]

BROTHER KEENAN:
   Right lads! Put away the books!
   There's two ways a' doing this,
   my way …
   Or the hard way!

   There's no one gonna give ya nothin' for nothin' in this world.
   D'ya hear me!
   The day of the job for life is gone!
   There's no shame in poverty!
   But 'tis nothin' to be proud of either.

Now, the view from the Northside is all fine and dandy.
Amn't I lookin' out from the Monastery meself every mornin'.
You can take it from me – it's a view that's hard to beat.

But I'll tell ya one thing about a view –
A view is one thing ya can't eat!
Ya can't heat a house with a view.
Ya can't put clothes on yer back with a view.

There's nothin' out there for ye!
No one's gonna give ye nothin' for nothin' in this world.
No one's gonna hand ye a job on a plate.
The day of a job for life is gone.

From now on – It's my way ...
Or the ...

[Transition: A snap transition back from BROTHER KEENAN to NARRATOR]

NARRATOR:
  ... hard way ...

And I thinkin' of Brother Keenan.
[Appears aggressive a sense of a surge of anger/fury rising up inside]

Like a ...
Like a wolf with a herd of sheep, he'd swoop,
select the most vulnerable and destroy.
And the sheep?
The sheep just huddled closer in silence.
[checks the time]

Twenty-two minutes 'til opening time.
Brother Keenan at the far end of French Church Street,
Standing between me an' the cure.
Headin' in my direction.

So, what do ya do?
What–do–ya–do?

Tell you what I did …
I set a course for a head-on collision.
That's what I did!

I'll kill him! I'll fuckin' well kill him!

V

And who pops his face up in front a' mine?
Only Timmy.
Timmy shaggin' Timmons.

TIMMY:

> [TIMMY's voice/high-pitched/ faux positive/ social climbing
> characteristics]
> Hi Ya!

NARRATOR:

> What can ya say to that? Hah? Nothin'!
> So I says nothing. Just look him up and down.
> He's standing there, the big polished face on him.
>
> Gold–rimmed glasses shinin',
> eyes twinklin' and smilin'.
> Standin' there in his full length, blue waxed cotton overcoat.
> Like an overgrown little Lord Fauntleroy.

Twenty-five years since I'd last set eyes on
Timmy shaggin' Timmons.
Didn't like him then – and not a lot has changed 'til now.

I'm tryin' to keep me eyes on Brother Keenan.
He's still way off in the distance.
Stopped outside Murray's gun shop.
Checkin' out the weapons,
no doubt.

Timmy shaggin' Timmons is tellin' me,
that I have just missed Mary ...

[Shrug shoulders – he doesn't know Mary]

TIMMY:

Mary? My missus!

NARRATOR:

Oh,
really disappointed –

Me hole!
He says that,
Mary's gone off to get his special Christmas present.
He's on the way to pick up somethin' special for her.

TIMMY:

It's a little thing we do every year!

NARRATOR:

Big – swingin' – mickey!

He's tellin' me that he has a little silversmith somewhere over
in the Wandsworth Quay who is making up a special ring for
her.

TIMMY:
>   Sam? Do you know Sam?

NARRATOR:
>   Eh? Sam? No, never heard of him …

TIMMY:
>   Sam the silversmith?
>   Ya must know Sam!
>   Everybody knows Sam!
>   Sam the silversmith?

NARRATOR:
>   He says something about,
>   two birthstones separated by a diamond.

>   – Wonderfil! says I.

>   And I'm just lookin' him up and down.
>   Everything is always *wonderfil*, with Timmy shaggin'
>   Timmons.
>   Two-faced Timmy, that's what I calls him.
>   Oh yeah, everybody loves,
>   Two-faced Timmy shaggin' Timmons.

>   I'm tryin' to keep an eye on Br Keenan at the far end a' the
>   street.
>   And, Two-faced Timmy's face is stuck in mine.

>   The last time the three of us –
>   Me, Two-faced Timmy shaggin' Timmons and Br Keenan
>   were in the same place,
>   the same shouting space,
>   must have been …
>   Must have been a lifetime ago.

Br Keenan, swoopin' around the classroom.
Timmy?
The fella with the pencil case …

Every type of pencil, biro, pen, marker, compass, divider, ruler,
set square and protractor you could think of.
The big shinin' face on him.
Always have the homework done – and he leapin' outa' his
desk.

[Hand darting up and down – attempting to attract the
attention of the teacher]

Br! Br! Br!
Br! Br! Br!

I mean, what the fuck was that all about?

If there weren't fellas like
Two-faced Timmy shaggin' Timmons in this world,
it'd be a damned site better place for fellas like me.
And I tell ya, dere's a lot a fellas like me …

VI

Fellas like Seánie Cronin.
Small Seánie – that's what we called him.
His dad hadn't worked in years,
I suppose for the best part of Small Seánie's short life.
Ma Cronin's nerves were bad, she had taken to the bed.
And probably because he had so much time on his hands,
Da Cronin took to porter.
Anyway, the upshot of the whole shebang was,
that Small Seánie was always late for school.
Well, half of the time anyway.

SEANIE:

[Schoolboy excuse /childlike voice]
Eh, the clock was stopped, Brother.

BROTHER KEENAN:

'Twas stopped then, was it, Seánín?

NARRATOR:

And he grabs Small Seánie by the ears,
lifts him clean off the floor –
and swings him towards de window.

[BROTHER KEENAN gesturing as if he has SEÁNIE held by the ear]

BROTHER KEENAN:

– Can ya see the clock on Shandon, Seánín?
Can ya! Well, Can ya!
Do you think I'm standin' up here day in day out,
for the good of me health!
Is that it, Seánín!
Is it! Hah? Is it!
Do you think I'm standin' up here just for the pleasure of yer
company?
Is that it, Seánín!
Standin' up here for the likes of you to stroll in and out when
ya please!
Is that it, Seánín!

Well let me tell you something for nothin'!
It don't matter to me if you're as thick as a ditch, boy!
It don't matter to me if you never learn to read or write.
It don't matter to me …
There's plenty fellas out there to take yer place on the factory
floor.

But if there's one thing you'll learn from me 'tis manners!
And if one fella like –
young Timmons there can be here on time every mornin'.
Then so can you!
Isn't that right, Seánín!

So, can ya see the clock on Shandon, Seánín!
And will ya see it in the mornin', you will?!
You won't forget to wind the clock tonight now will ya?!
Hah?! Seánín?! Hah!?
'Tis my way or the hard way …

[As Brother Keenan releases his grip – in his transition to the
Narrator he momentarily becomes Seánie – and squeals in
pain]

Narrator:
Seánie squealed,
Brother Keenan smiled
and the sheep giggling nervously, huddled closer.

Two-faced Timmy shaggin' Timmons is still talkin'.
He's talkin' about his kids.
Tírnán, Róisín and Facthna …

[Sarcastic exaggerated Irish pronunciation of names]

Tírnán, Róisín and Fachtna?
I mean what the fuck is that all about?!

What's wrong with normal names?
Names like - Mick, Paddy or Mary.
Do ya know what's wrong with 'em?
I'll tell ya what's wrong with 'em!
They're not good enough!

They're not good enough for Two-faced Timmy shaggin'
Timmons!
No way!

Oh, no –
since Two-faced Timmy shaggin' Timmons left our street
and moved to leafy suburbia,
a lot of things aren't good enough for him.
It's better to have kids with names ya can't pronounce out
where he lives.
It's like Irish is the language of the new middle classes.

He asks me,

TIMMY:
> *[Irish pronunciation of Cáitlín is exaggerated]*
> How's Cáitlín?

NARRATOR:
> *[Confused look]*
> Cáitlín, who?

TIMMY:
> Cáitlín your wife.

NARRATOR:
> Oh, Kathleen?

And I'm thinkin' to meself –
How the fuck am I supposed to know how Kathleen is,
I've been on the batter for three days.

Eh? She's fine Timmy. She's at home stuffin' the turkey.

And I offers him a fag.

TIMMY:

No thanks, I don't smoke!

NARRATOR:

Typical, bloody well typical!
He says he's gotta rush, but that …

TIMMY:

We must meet sometime for a jar.

NARRATOR:

[Cynical laugh]
A jar?
Yeah Right!

Merry Christmas, he says.

And then, wait for it, – *Slán!*
In his broadest Bun Tús Cainte Irish, – Sláaan!
And he walks off, leaving me standin' there,
cigarette in me hand.

VII

Brother Keenan at the far end of the street,
still checkin' out the weapons.
My mind is reelin',
I'm not really sure if today is the right day –
for me to be comin' face to face with my past.
I mean, Jesus, today of all days.
God-almighty, I'm just out lookin' for a cure –
And by Christ, do I need a cure.

Pools of dirty black water –

splashin' up at me from under cracked and battered pavement.
So I steps into a doorway, lights up me damp John Player Blue,
'cause I'm soaked –
absolutely soaked from me head right down to me feet.

And I'm standin' there on the side a the street,
Numbskulled and thinkin'.
Thinkin', watchin' and sinkin'.
Sinkin' down to me oxters, puffin' on a fag,
tryin' to catch me breath.

[Hissed/whispered]
Two-faced Timmy shaggin' Timmons, hah?

Jesus!
Somebody famous once said that life is like a train journey.
Well if life's a train journey.
It's amazing,
how me and Two-faced Timmy shaggin' Timmons
got on at the same station,
and ended up in two totally different places.

He was always fuckin' strange anyway.
Even when we were young fellas,
the big polished face of him –
and his mam tellin' him to stay in outa' the street …

TIMMY'S MOTHER:
    Timmy! Stay away from them, Timmy boy!
    They'll only drag ya down into the gutter with them!

NARRATOR:
    Away from us? Away from us!
    I mean what the fuck is that all about!

[As if peering out from doorway]

No budge outa' Brother Keenan.
He's still standin' there outa' focus.

So, I'm slinkin' in me doorway, suckin' on a damp fag.

Up the street, outside the bookshop,
The Butter Exchange Band.
Are tuning up to play …

[SFX: Fade up brass band tuning up – into the opening riff of – Bleak Mid Winter.]

VIII

So, I'm sittin' there, squattin' and thinkin',
in a doorway on French Church Street.
And I closes me eyes.

Closes me eyes, throws back me head.
And d'ya know what?
I sing along …

[At this point NARRATOR sings In Bleak Mid Winter. He's not a performance singer – it's as if he's singing in a garbled way to himself and it brings him back to another time. He hums the words he doesn't know and adds a bit of ad-lib composition. The volume of the band fades and the monologue continues.]

[sing]
In d'bleak mid-winter,
frosty winds may blow …
[makes up garbled the words of next two lines]

Snow had fallen, snow or snow,
Snowy snowy snow – [incorrect words]
In d'bleak mid-winter
Long time ago …

[contd.]

… somethin' about Christmas carols that'd get the head
spinnin'.
And I'm thinkin' about Kathleen.
Kathleen and the kids.
It's always been me and Ka,
Ka and me – ever since we were kids.

… there was a time.
Just outa' school.
Seen Rolf Harris on the telly.
Got it int've me head –
Gonna go to the far side of the world.

Australia –
half of Cork was down there.
Plenty a' work, plenty a' money.
One-way ticket to the sunshine.
Get the fuck outa' this crumblin' port town,
outa' this, this, mullet-ville.

BROTHER KEENAN:
> *My way or the hard way?*

NARRATOR:
> Fuck that for a game a' darts!
> From now on it was gonna be the easy way,
> or no way at all!
> Everything hunky-dory.
> Had the medical, the passport photos, the visa, the lot.

Said me goodbyes to Second City.
Last smell of the river Lee.
Said me good byes to Ka.
On me way to Australi-aa.

I was on me way to where the sun shines.
On me way to make some hay.

[Sing]
Tie me kangaroo down, sport.
Tie me kangaroo down.
Everybody now.
Tie me kangaroo down, sport.
Tie me kangaroo …

That's when Ka dropped a bombshell.
Baby on the way …

Well any plans I had of swimmin' with Flipper –
Or goin' on the hop with Skippy,
were chucked in the river that day.

And they all said it would never last!
Yeah, well, I proved them wrong! Didn't I!
I stuck around!
A lot of fellas would have fucked off!
But I stuck around!
Mightn't be a match made in heaven.
But sink or swim – it was a match made in Cork.
And - Jesus I stuck around.

And ya be lookin' at the telly,
and ya be gettin' a glimpse,
of what Christmas is like for other people.

But it's never like that though – is it?
I mean Christmas is just the same as any other time a the year.
'Cept?
'Cept there's more of it.
More eatin', more drinkin', more spendin', more shoutin', more roarin', more fightin' …

Then again?
Then again …
It hasn't been right.
It hasn't been right for a long time, between me and Ka, like?
'Twasn't always that way …

There was a time – there was a time when me and Ka were like …

[Two fingers clenched together]
Like, that la!

She was my lady. I was her man.
Some woman all the same.
Use'ta love her pint an all. Mad for road! Mad for road!
Karaoke? Jez she'd set the place on fire.
The Karaoke queen of Blackpool, so she was.
Lived for it – every Friday night – out in Hally's
She'd take the mic.
Be a star – my star …

[Sudden Transition to Karaoke Club – NARRATOR walks to specific location]
[LX: karaoke club effect – Mirror Ball]
[Sing karaoke style, amateur night 'workingman's club-esque' – slightly OTT – maybe slight reverb.
He's moving and gesturing as if singing in a night club – pointing to the audience – and winking at girls in the crowd etc. He hums the words

he doesn't know and adds a bit of ad-lib composition – and of course he knows the last two words – 'The Power of Love' so he gives those two words a big 'power' finish.]

'Cause I am your lay-dee,
and you are my ma-ah-ah-an …

Whenever you reach for meeee
I'll do all that I can.

We're heading for something
Somewhere I've never been
Sometimes da-da da-da
Da-da-da-a learn
De power of loveeee

And they loved her.
I loved her.
Lived for her.
Lived for each other –
Lived for Friday night –
Used to get on like a?
Like a house on fire …

House on fire?! *[Cynical]*
There's no point callin' the fire brigade to our gaff.
Not now anyway.
'Cause that fire's well and truly gone out at this stage …

Jez,
'Tis the kids!
'Tis the kids that I blames!

'Twas like all of a sudden she got all serious like.
I mean, these days? What once was – is well and truly gone.

And maybe? Maybe sometimes drink does get in the way.
No doubt, I do like me pint –
But I always liked me pint.

And I be lookin' at these experts on the telly.
And they tellin' me that fellas who drinks or takes drugs and
all that,
be doin' it cause there's somethin' missin' in their lives.

Missing in their lives?
Well, let me tell you something for nothin'.
There's nothin' missin' in my life, thank you very much!
If anythin', if anythin',
I has more now – than I ever had before.

'cause these days I has three kids on top of everything else –
And you can take it from me,
women changes after they has kids …

And one thing I've learned about relationships –

When the chemistry goes in a relationship –
There's nothin' for it –
But to take more chemicals!

[Checks time again]
12 minutes 'til opening time.
I'm lookin' out from the shelter, happy as Larry Kearney.
And I'm singin', just singin' a song in the rain.

[NARRATOR - continues singing, Bleak Mid Winter' – with ad-lib composition]
snowey, snowey, snowey snow
snowey snowey, snow,
In d'bleak mid-wi …

[Narrator singing stops abruptly – reacts as if somebody has bumped off him]

IX

[Narrator moves as if he has been bumped – angry reaction]

What the fuck! Swear to God!

And out he steps from the door behind me.
Out into the rain, all dressed up for the weather.

And to make matters worse – as he pushes his way past,
he presses a two euro coin into me hand.

– Happy Christmas! says he.

Two euro? Two fuckin' euro?
And me with a hundred and fifty a' the fuckin' things in me
arse pocket.

– Hoi! I'm no beggar!

I don't know whether to say thanks or give him a dig!
But he's gone!

And as I look around me,
I realises that I'm not shelterin' in any ol' doorway.
Naw, naw, naw, naw, naw …
Not at all …

I'm standin' on a well-worn granite step,
surrounded by the red and white of Cork.
An arch of cut limestone and sandstone –

The side door to St Peter and Paul's.

And I hear someone shout,

– *Hoi! Fuck off home to where ya came from!*

– *Who me! [or react aggressively]*

A fraction of a second before I realise they're not shoutin' at
me at all,
but at this Romanian woman.
She's crouched there along side me.
Big and colourful.
Dazzling half the street with a mouthful of grinnin' gold teeth.
And she squattin' there along-side me shelterin'.
Sellin' *Big Issues* –
Shelterin' under the outstretched arms of a God she don't even
believe in.

– *How's it goin'?*

ROMANIAN WOMAN:
   Big Issue! Big Issue …

NARRATOR:
   Yerrah! Fuck *Big Issue!*

                           X

Now,
I haven't set foot inside a church in a lifetime.
And a lifetime is a long time.

A lifetime?
[Inspires memory]

Like a, like a job for life.
Like, my father had a job for life – that was a long time.

My father?
The hub of the household – my father.

*['The Hub of The Household' needs to be impressed on the audience –
maybe a hand gesture – such as a hub of a wheel – this becomes relevant
when the phrase takes on a different interpretation later in the play]*

Down the Marina, keepin' the wheels of industry turnin',
For Henry Ford Motor Works.
A job for life? For fuck sake!

Don't mind yer job for life – it was a job for generations.
Where a workplace was handed down from father to son.
And I'd be next in line – for me place on the assembly line.

Transition: from NARRATOR *to* FATHER. FATHER *is older so maybe his
frame is slightly more hunched / voice deeper / slower.*
FATHER *– a working class man with a simplistic view of life – a man
born into the 'Job for Life' generation]*

FATHER:
Ya won't do better than Fords, Son. –'Tis a job for …

NARRATOR:
Don't say it, Dad!

FATHER:
But 'tis …
'Tis a job for …

NARRATOR:
I don't want to hear about it, Dad.

FATHER:

No hear me out, Son!
… a job for …

NARRATOR:

No, Dad … No …

FATHER:

… for life!

NARRATOR:

Ah Jesus!

FATHER:

And Henry Ford is a true son of Cork –
and when he made it big over there in America –
he never forgot where he came from, did he?
Not at all!
Of all the cities in all the world,
he set up his factory here in Cork down the Marina.

So that generations of Cork men,

Men like you and me, Son,
would never have to work again.

The man was a genius!
Not only did he invent the motorcar –
but he invented what's known as – The job for …

NARRATOR:

Don't say it, Dad!

FATHER:

Job for …

NARRATOR:

No, Dad! No!

FATHER:

Job for life!

NARRATOR:

Ah, Jeezus, Dad!

Well it was a job for life, *[sarcastic]*
until they shut the fuckin' place down.
And the funny thing is –
the day me dad stopped workin' …
was the day he stopped livin'.

Now there's a job for life!
He didn't die or nothing, not at all. Naw, naw, naw …
He just stopped!
Stopped drinking, stopped smoking, stopped the horses,
stopped going to Mass, stopped goin' to football …

Sur' Jesus, he even gave his dog away!
Stopped bringing his dog for a walk.
Just gave up!
Stopped!
Stopped dead!

[Moment of realisation – big statement]
And that's when my dad became –
The hub of the household.

[Once again 'Hub of the Household' is impressed on the audience – maybe uses hand movement to explain the principle of the wheel]

'Cause anyone who knows anythin'

about the fundamental principles of the wheel will tell ya –
That while that wheel is turning,
and the spokes and outer rim are spinnin' around and round
like be Jazus …
The hub?
The hub is locked solid at the centre –
Locked solid and does not move.

Like me dad, without a budge out of him.
Livin' off the bit of redundancy,
making do with whatever few bob me mam pulled in from the
cleaning.

He wasn't long changin' his tune then though.
Oh no …

FATHER:

Now that Fords and Dunlops are gone, Son –
you'll just have to follow yer nose …

NARRATOR:

Follow me nose, Dad?
That's some fuckin' career path!

FATHER:

It's the way of the future, Son …
Even the government are sayin' it!
We'll all have to tighten our belt
and follow our noses.
The day of the job for life is gone, boy!
There's nothin' out there for ya!

NARRATOR:

And Brother Keenan then with his …

BROTHER KEENAN:*[reverb]*

> There's nothin' out there for ye!
> No one's gonna give ye nothin' for nothin' in this world.
> No one's gonna hand ye a job on a plate.
> The day of a job for life is gone.
> From now on,
> It's my way or the …

NARRATOR:

> … Hard way …
> And up to that point,
> I was secure in the knowledge of a job for life.
> And just like that –
> the rug is pulled out from under me.
>
> I mean, no doubt, my dad was caught on the hop.
> And Brother Keenan? He didn't know which way to look.
> But all they could do,
> was to spout out meaningless shite –
> And educate me for the dole queue.

BROTHER KEENAN: *[reverb]*

> It's all about power – power and control.
> And no man can give you power.
> Do ya hear me!
> No man can give ya power!
> Power's something ya gotta reach out and take for yerself!
> It's survival of the fittest out there.
> Kill or be killed. Dog eat dog.
>
> 'Cause fellas like ye haven't a prayer.
> 'Tis my way or the hard way!
> The view from the Northside will pay no bills.
> Ya got to drop yer sights,
> take what's goin'…

We'll educate ye for the dole …
Me hole!

XI

And I am standing in the doorway of St. Peter and Paul's.
And just around the corner? Christmas.
And I'm lookin' out on Second City,
mind the dog shit,
turd town.
With all these Celtic Tiger Cubs,
with their mobile phones, and laptops.
Bottled water, backpacks, i-pods and belly tops …

Goin' to the College of Art and Design. *[sarcastic/pretentious accent]*
Goin' to be a designer.
With their PhD in some class of technology.
And they lookin' at me like I'm a dinosaur.

With me cert from ANCO or Fás –
or whatever the fuck they calls it these days.

And maybe they're right.
Maybe I am a dinosaur in this land of plenty.
But my future was written on the wall,
a long time ago – when there was sweet fuck-all …

Now, I've two choices.
One! I stand here being dazzled by the Rumanian,
being mistaken for a beggar.
Or, B! I go back out under the rain – face Brother Keenan
down …

So what do ya do?! What do ya do?!

Do ya know what I did?
I'll tell ya what I did.

I opens the door behind me –
And follows me nose into the house of God instead.

XII

[LX: Inside church – LX: stained glass gobo.]
[SFX: Haunting sound of hand held bells chiming the tune of 'In The Bleak Mid Winter]

[Give NARRATOR *some time to get his bearings – he is looking around the church obviously feeling a bit uncomfortable to be inside a church]*

[Deep inhale through nose]
First thing?
The first thing that hits me is the …
Is the?
I'm not too sure what it is.
Somethin' ya can't really put a finger on.
A bit like, a bit like God.

And that's exactly what it is.
It's the scent of God.
Like a musty, dusty blending – of incense and candle wax,
floor polish and wine.

And I'm standing there,
[deep inhale] just takin' it all in …

Checkin' out the locals,

and I can see by the look in their eyes –
they know that I'm no regular.

To me right, a fella about twenty – twenty stone like.
And his head thrown back and he snoring' like a tractor.

To the left of me, a woman with her shoes off,
Tesco bags piled up all 'round her,
like she's manning the barricades.

There's a man over there in a flat cap.
Or is it his hair?
He's doin' the Stations of the Cross –
with a little black and tan terrier on a rope …

At the scourging of Christ –
where the Romans had the Son of Man,
stripped naked to the navel and whippin' him.
The terrier cocks his leg –
empties his bladder against the pew.

Hard to know if he's taking his revenge on the Romans –
or the Roman Catholics…

– *You tell 'em Shep! You tell 'em!*

Says the man in the cap.
Or is it his hair?

At the side altar, there's an auld wan – and she stretched out.
Stretched out on the ground and she mutterin' to herself.
talkin' all s-es - you know like …

[Action/ blessing herself, feverishly, sound of old women whispering prayers]

– Psss, pss, ps, psss, pss, ps, psss, pss, ps ...

Tellin' ya?
This would be would be some pub if they sold drink!

Hand cut tiles,
terrazzo flooring, mosaic walls,
velvet crushed by the generations of genuflecting faithful.
Brass and copper trimmings on blood red mahogany.
Pink Italian marble pillars rising up to the heavens.
Statues of angels and saints, holy men and women.
Images of Gods poppin' up all over the gaff.
The full three generations of Jesus' extended family for Christ's
sake!

Paintin's and pictures. Pictures of the most degrading torture –
carried out by man on the Son of Man.
And altars? Altars groaning under the guilt (gilt) of gold.

And all this is tinted by a haze of burgundies, blues and
purples
filtering through spotless stained glass.

And everything ...
Everything sparkling under the flickerin' flame of a thousand
candles.

God al-mighty!
'Tis like Aladdin's cave – on acid.

[Checks time]
10 minutes 'til openin' time –
So I sits down,
two rows up from the woman with the no shoes and the
shoppin'.

She's just sittin' there thinkin'.
Just like me …
She's – shelterin' from the pain – and the rain – and the street.

XIII

[NARRATOR takes a few moments to get into the zone – maybe fade up the sound of hand held bells of – Bleak Mid-Winter]

And I'm thinkin' …
Thinkin' of Brother Keenan …

I mean, he knew that my mam and dad fought like cat and dog.
Everybody knew.
Don't get me wrong –
There was no shame in it.
There was no harm in it.
That's how they got on.

But, I'd be up half the night listening to the carry-on down in the kitchen.
And there was no real harm in it.
But t'was hard to sleep through.

Brother Keenan –
spoutin' on about the Modh Coinníollach or the Tuiseal Ginideach or somethin'… I'm keeled over, head down on the desk – asleep.

Like a soaring vulture,
Brother Keenan's hand cast a shadow over the back of me bowl-cut pole and, with a roar of,

BROTHER KEENAN: *[reverb]*
    Wake up, man!

NARRATOR:
    His manly hand crushed a clatter into me ear,
    a clatter that lifted me clean out of me desk
    and into the middle of the following week.
    Landed in a heap – up against the wall, under the shadow of
    the Virgin.

BROTHER KEENAN:
    – You look more comfortable there, man. You can stay there!

NARRATOR:
    The sheep closed ranks and I stayed where I was,
    kneeling by me desk for the rest of that day.
    I slept that night – I'm tell ya that much.

    And I'm sittin' and thinkin'…
    And when yer sittin' there in silence – it's hard not to think.
    Especially when the only interruption to yer thoughts –
    is the sound of a penny drop –
    in the poor box.
    I'm thinkin' of my father.

XIV

FATHER:
    Not easy!?
    What do you know about not easy, Son?
    I'll tell you about not easy.
    Don't get me wrong now,
    but my father, your Grandfather had a good job.
    Suppose you could say it was a – a job for …

NARRATOR:

Don't say it, Dad! Don't say it!

FATHER:

… for life.

NARRATOR:

Ah, Jesus!

FATHER:

– Yer Grandfather followed his nose to work day–in day–out,
year–in year–out.
[rapid fire] Past the cattle out in the dealers' field,
past the pubs, the bakeries, the toffee-making shawlies,
the distillery, the slaughterhouse, the tannery,
the sweet factory all the way to the first trace of human waste
at Poulraddy.

NARRATOR:

Yeah, yeah, I've heard it all before, Dad!

FATHER:*[sniff]*

But Jesus, one mornin' …
One mornin' and he turnin' into Leitrim Street by Murphy's
brewery
[inhale through nose]
it didn't smell right.
Didn't smell right at all!

Like the smell a' death.
Choking him.
'Twas like, like a, like a, like a, burnin' mattress …
That's what it was like.

He didn't close his eyes
and whistle his way to the Three Points Corner that mornin'.
He had to keep his eyes open 'cause the tell–tale scents along
the way
were masked by an overpowering stench of damp smoulderin'
smoke.
So thick to make his eyes water.
At Falvey's corner he hesitated,
expecting to hit the familiar wall of fish from the Baltimore
Stores –
But not a trace.

Not as much as a Tárnín.
There was no point him looking back at Shandon,
'cause the smoke was that thick – he couldn't see beyond his
nose.
So he stepped onto Bridge Street – just hoping …
Hopin' for that familiar scent of fine wine and exotic spices
from Madden's…

But Jesus, what your Grandda saw that mornin' stopped him
in his tracks.

'Twas like something from Dante's Inferno.
Devastation heaped on destruction.
Not one stone left standing on another.
His beautiful city, burnt to the ground!
Burnt to the ground by the Black and Tans.

And I says to your Grandfather,
I says, Dad, ya must have seen it comin'?
I mean Jesus, the town was a powder keg,
Two Lord Mayors murdered, stone dead.
One in Brixton Prison and one shot in the head.
A langer load a' Brits wiped out in Kilmichael.

The Delany brothers shot dead in their beds.
Week after week of reprisal and counter-reprisal.
And ya didn't see it comin'?!

No!

I mean Jesus, yer Grandfather might have been walkin' round
the town with his eyes closed but he wasn't a blind man.
He knew what was going on!
He knew the town was about to explode.
Hunger strikes, executions,
The Cork Brigade sloggin' it out on every street corner!
You can be dammed sure he knew what was goin' on.
But rather bury his head in the sand.
Rather walk around with his eyes closed.
And you're the same, Son!

NARRATOR:
I'm the same? What about you, Dad!
The hub of the household since Fords closed!

FATHER:
Look, all I'm sayin' is –
that girl is pregnant and you better do the right thing by her!
You can't just close yer eyes and pretend it's not happenin'!
Ya can't just walk away!
I seen it before!

NARRATOR:
You've seen it before, Dad?!
Did ya ever try lookin' at yer self!

FATHER:
Let me finish, boy. Let me finish!
The first thing that crossed your Grandda's mind when he saw

the city smouldering that morning – was not –
that the British had levelled his town. Not at all …

The first thing that crossed yer Grandda's mind was,
that deep down under that pile of smoking debris –

his job was dead and buried.

And he just gave up!
And while any other man would have heard the call to arms,
or at least would have went out and found another job.

Do ya know what yer Grandda did? I'll tell ya what he did …

He walked straight across the street to Crowley's pub
and called himself a pint of porter.
[slight sarcastic laugh] A pint a' porter!?
Sat there at the bar in Crowley's for three years.

Three whole years!

Drank his way right through the War of Independence and
the Civil War –
so he did.
And after truce and treaty.
And all the old scores were settled,
there was nothing for him to do –
but to drink some more …

So don't you talk to me about – not easy, boy.
What the fuck would you know about –
Not easy …

XV

NARRATOR:
> So I'm sitting here in St. Peter and Paul's and I'm thinking …
> Sins of the father – sins of the son.
> Like a legacy – handed down from generation to generation…
>
> Like a baton in a relay race.
> And I'm thinkin' of my Grandda,
> A man who'd rather walk around the town followin' his nose,
> with his eyes closed – than face reality.
> And I'm thinkin' of me father – stopped dead like the hub in a
> wheel.
> And I'm thinkin' of …
> I'm thinkin' of …
> I'm thinkin' of me.
> Me and Kathleen.
> And I'm thinkin'…

XVI

> *[Checks Time]*
> Six minutes 'til openin' time, so I head for the street and a
> cure.
> And by Christ do I need a cure.
>
> Rain stopped.
> Sun out.
> I dowse meself with a handful a holy water.
> Throws a splash on the Rumanian as well, for good measure.
> She smiles. I'm caught 'tween the sunlight and the glare of her
> teeth.

ROMANIAN WOMAN:
>
> Big Issue, Big Issue …

NARRATOR:
>
> So I steps out. Back out onto French Church Street.
> And there, no more than a couple a feet,
> still heading in my direction – that bastard of a man,
> Brother Keenan.
>
> like a trapped animal,
> Hairs stiffening to a ridge along the back of me neck.
> Teeth grinding, knuckles whitened – frightened.
> Pace slow.
> His face comin' into focus.
>
> Right hand slips from my pocket,
> in preparation for retribution. [Maybe delete this line?]
>
> Brother Keenan, not two yards from me.
> I raise my elbow.
> The plan is simple.
> One quick clatter int'v his ear.
> Sorted!
>
> But outa' the blue, outa' the blue,
> just as he drew alongside –
> he out manoeuvres me and stops.
>
> Called out my name?

[We now meet BROTHER KEENAN in real life rather than as an expression of NARRATOR's memory – he is not as terrifying as previously presented. He is elderly and slightly unsteady and feeble. It gradually becomes apparent that the smile on his face is more a pained smile than a smile of terror]

BROTHER KEENAN:
Ó Murchú?

NARRATOR:
His cheeks stretch to a smile, a smile I had learned to fear.
But in a funny sort a way I'm flattered.

I mean, at one stage or another,
Brother Keenan must have had nearly every downtown dirty
face from across the Northside a' the city
– standin' in his shadow.
And here, here on French Church Street, after all these years,
he recognises me?

BROTHER KEENAN:
Cíarán Ó Murchú, nach ea?

NARRATOR: [sarcastic laugh]
He thinks I'm my older brother Ciaran.
– Ní hea, a bhráthar, ach Seán.

BROTHER KEENAN:
Ah, conas atá tú, a Sheáin?

NARRATOR:
How are ya Seán? How are ya indeed?
Why am I speaking Irish to this tyrant?
'Tis the language he terrorised me with!

My mind's reelin' and I don't really know if I'm ready for this.
I'm just out lookin' for a cure, and by Christ do I need a cure!
But by some twisted deal of fate,
I'm dealin' with this?

He's standing there smilin' – so I answer him …

– Eh, I'm fine, Brother. How're you?

And then he starts …

XVII

BROTHER KEENAN:
>   Ah sure, I'm retired now. I miss de old days.
>   I miss de boys.
>   …the good old days.

NARRATOR:
>   Goodolddays? Goodolddays, me hole!
>   And without taking a breath, he's off talkin' …

BROTHER KEENAN:
>   Yourself, Cíarán and Pádraig got on famously.
>   God bless ye, I always knew ye would.

NARRATOR:
>   Just waiting for a gap in the gobble-de-gook,
>   so I can stretch out a clatter into his ear.
>   But, he's still rambling on.

[NARRATOR gradually becomes aware that BROTHER KEENAN is no longer to be feared. He is now an infirm elderly man]

>   And I'm standin' there lookin' him up an' down.
>   Watery eyes rolling between wrinkled lids.
>   His skin about two sizes too big for him.
>   'Tis like he's after shrinkin' or somethin'.
>   Then again, it's been a long time –
>   maybe I've …

[NARRATOR struggles with the idea that he is not the small boy anymore]

His collar looser, hair grey and wispy.
Skin old and worn, body bent and tired.
He's chunterin' on about – *the good ol' days …*

BROTHER KEENAN:
Ah sur' God in heaven,
the monastery was like a beehive in them days.
More Brothers than you could shake a stick at.
'Twas a real community, a community in the community.

Sur' there's only a handful of us left now…

And the monastery is gone!
Who would think it – levelled to the ground …
Gone, gone, gone …

And I tell ya 'twas no coincidence –
that the fall off in hurling on the Northside of the city
happened
at the same time as the fall off in vocations to the Brothers.

See the Brothers had very little.
Gave up everything so we did.
Everything for a life of poverty, celibacy and prayer.
We had very little of anything – anything but time.
And time was the one thing we had plenty of.

Time for the boys –
Sur' who else would be bringin' 'em up the field,
to flake a sliotar around the place?
Hah? Hah? Who else?
Keepin' 'em out of trouble.
Who else? Hah!

Ah, they were the good ol' days!

NARRATOR:

And he's chunterin' on.
Chunterin' on like a man who'd just been relieved of a
lifetime's vow of silence.
He's talkin' about my brothers,
Ciaran and Paddy, their wives, their children, their lives.
The detail is frightening.
He mentions names,
names of boys I can't put faces to.

BROTHER KEENAN:

Ah, Jesus, you must remember him!
You must! A big lump of a fella!
You remember him alright, ya do!
A right blackguards - always in trouble.
Ya must remember him…

NARRATOR:

No, Brother …

BROTHER KEENAN:

Big fella! Ah Jesus ya do!
Big fella!
Went on to be the commissioner in the Guards!
Retired now…

NARRATOR:

Retired?!
Eh? I'd say he was in a different year to me, Brother?

BROTHER KEENAN:

…and sur' what about yer man?
The fella with the hair?
You know who I'm talking about…

NARRATOR:
[Confused look]

BROTHER KEENAN:
Ah, ya do, ya do!
Ya know him alright!
The musician!
[Clumsy air-guitar]
The musician with the hair!
You know him. Ah, ya do!
The fella with the hair!

NARRATOR:
Eh? Rory Gallagher, Brother?

BROTHER KEENAN:
The very man!
Sur' he went on to great things, God bless him.
Although tell ya the truth,
Personally, I never really could make head nor tail of that
Rock and Roll thing.
But I tell ya an odd one now – I always loved dancin'!

NARRATOR:
Dancin', Brother?

BROTHER KEENAN:
I always loved to dance, so I did …

NARRATOR:
And I'm havin' this weird vision of all these Christian Brothers
–
dressed up in black and they movin' and grovin'
and dancin' the night away around the monastery…

BROTHER KEENAN:

    Don't get me wrong now,
    I only danced once in me life
    and that was the day of my sister's wedding.
    Danced me feet off, so I did.
    'Twas the most fun I've ever had.
    All my aunts and the women of the street telling me that I was
    a great dancer – for a Christian Brother.

    Yes, *[contemplative]* I danced that day so I did…

    Actually I lie,
    I danced twice in me life.
    On the night of me mother's funeral,
    I danced with me sister around the kitchen at home.
    She said, Mammy would have wanted it – for she knew how
    much I enjoyed the dancing at the wedding.

[Words recited to the rhythm of a barn dance – maybe clapping his hand to the beat]

    Didn't they draw back the table…
    And all the family, and friends, and neighbours banged out a
    tune
    clapping their hands
    and stampin' their feet –
    and meself and me sister –
    we danced –
    Danced and danced 'til dawn – so we did.
    Round the kitchen and mind the dresser.
    Danced and danced 'til dawn so we did …

    Even to this very day –
    whenever I hear the right music on the wireless –
    can't help it, but don't the feet get to tapping.
    Great days all the same …

XVIII

NARRATOR:

    He's talking of the hurling and football greats.
    And beaming with pride, a fatherly pride,
    Brother Keenan is standing there in front of me,
    filing through the pages of the lives of statesmen,
    businessmen, sportsmen …

    – *My boys,* he calls them. – *My boys* …

    And he stands there smiling.

BROTHER KEENAN:

    – Different days, now, hah!?
    'Tis all joyridin' and drugs with them these days, hah?!
    There's no controlin' them now.
    'Tis the parents I blames – too soft they're gone altogether.
    What these young gurriers need is a good clip in the ear.
    And that would sort 'em out.
    As I always says – a clip in time saves?

NARRATOR:

    Eh? Nine, Brother?

BROTHER KEENAN:

    That's right – a clip in time saves nine!

    But, no, no regrets.
    They were the good ol' *days.*
    [pause]
    And I suppose if I did have any regrets …
    It'd be only the one. One small regret …
    [change to reflective]
    … sometimes I wonder what it might have been like to have
    been married?

NARRATOR:
>   Married?

BROTHER KEENAN:
>   Y'know, a wife …
>   and maybe – children of my own?
>   I often wondered what it might be like – to be called Dad …
>   Y'know – instead of Brother …

NARRATOR: *[taken aback by* BROTHER KEENAN'S *regret]*
>   One small regret? One small regret!
>
>   To live his days on the outside lookin' in?
>   Like a kid with his nose pressed against a toyshop window.
>   Wonderin' – What if? What if?
>   Ya can't live a life of what ifs?
>
>   *[reflective: sing quietly – almost a whisper]*
>   Tie me kangaroo down sport.
>   Tie me kangaroo down…
>   everybody now…

BROTHER KEENAN:
>   Ah, but sur', the Brothers?
>   The Brothers are my family.
>   And the lads?
>   The lads are – my boys.
>   My boys …
>
>   Ye were great lads, so ye were …
>   And I think of ye,
>   I do. I think of ye all – all the time.

NARRATOR:

Brother Keenan smiles and nods his head and makes to pass by.

XIX

Enough of this gibberish, the time for talk is over.
And just as he draws level,
I raise my elbow to shoulder height.
Ready to give him one clean smack into the ear.

– Brother Keenan?!

BROTHER KEENAN:
– Seán?

NARRATOR:

And for the first time, I can see his smile – is a smile of pain.
Brother Keenan's pain.
Like the pain of a parent …
Or somethin'…
[Shaking himself out of it]
Jesus, I dunno?!
I dunno.
Me mind's doin' somersaults …

– Seán? he says it again.
[Raises his arm as if about to hit him – but hesitates and takes stock of what he's about to do]

… hand dipped to waist height …
[choice to use previous line or act as a moment of intense turmoil/ confusion]

[confused, slightly emotional – he stretches out his hand to shake hands]

– ehhm, Happy Christmas, Brother Keenan.

BROTHER KEENAN:
> – Nollaig faoi mhaise duit, a Sheáin …

NARRATOR:
> My grip eases on his soft chalky fingers –
> and slowly he shuffles off.

XX

NARRATOR:
> I stand there watchin',
> my once-in-a-lifetime chance to even all the odds, just …
> Just walkin' away.
>
> My right hand knotted to a fist
> and I grind it down –
> into the palm of my left.
>
> And I'm standin' there on French Church Street just two
> minutes to the cure.
>
> In the horrors …
> And after generations of closed eyes, walkin' away and shiftin'
> the blame…
>
> Here I am,
> alone in the rain
> with no one to blame,
> but me.

– Go after him.
Let him go.
One flake into the head!
No!

I watch Brother Keenan as he shuffles off,
'til he fades away into the loneliness,
back to his own heaven or hell – I'll never know.

Brother Keenan turns into Paul Street.
And I just stand there watching …
Watching as he shuffles away – out of my life forever.

XXI

It was a sleepy Saturday morning on Halfmoon Street,
and just around the corner – Christmas.
I was walking off a bit of self-inflicted pain, you know how it
is?
Three days on the ran-tan,
Three days drinkin' my severance bonus.

Too much goin' on me mind, head full of noise.
Seagulls squawkin', hawkers hawkin' –

like a kango hammer right between me eyes,
drillin' a hole int'v me brain.

The soles of me shoes pushin' pavement,
like they were tappin' out time.
Tappin' out time 'til the pubs opened.
Then I'd go back in for the cure.
And by Christ, did I need a cure…

But didn't fate took a hand to my feet,
turned them into French Church Street.

So, I turned on my heels …

Turned on my heels.
Turned on my heels and went home.

The pain?
The pain was still there.

But the cure?

The cure had set in.

[SFX: Fade out with Brass Band playing 'Going Home']

[LX: Bring up silhouette of NARRATOR *against red backdrop – echoing the opening scene.]*
[LX: Fade to Black]

THE END

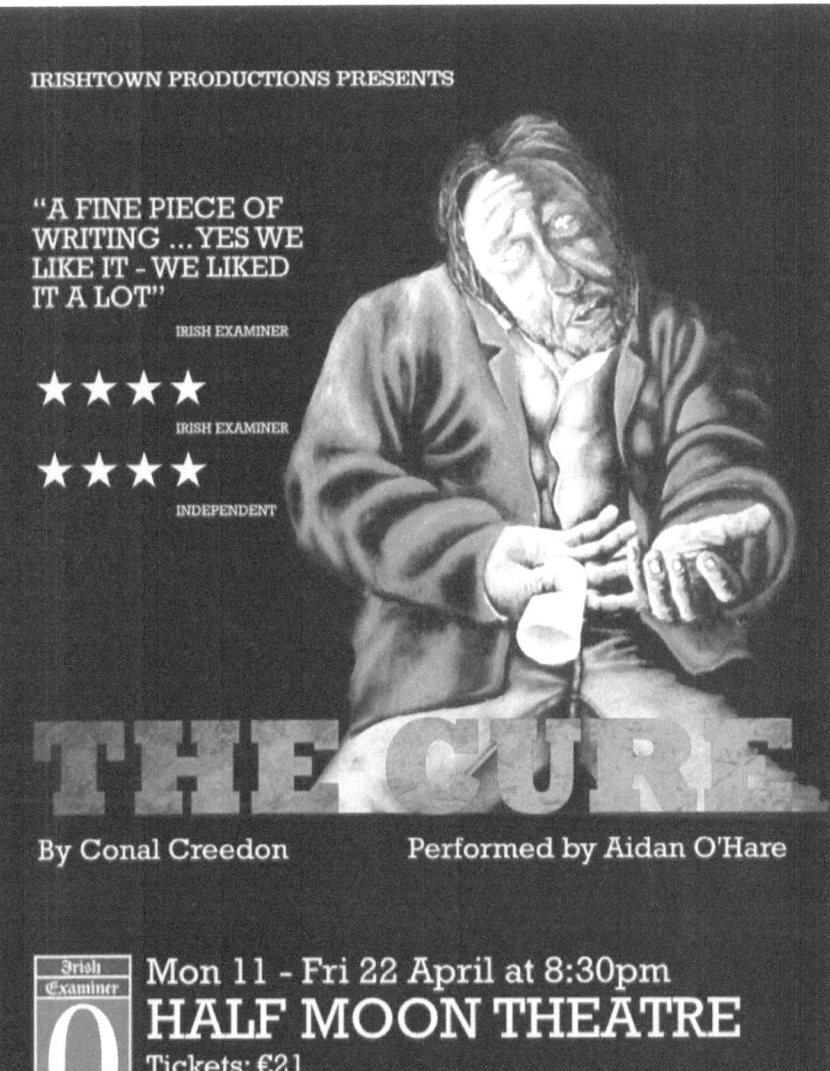

IRISHTOWN PRODUCTIONS PRESENTS

"A FINE PIECE OF WRITING ... YES WE LIKE IT - WE LIKED IT A LOT"

IRISH EXAMINER

★★★★

IRISH EXAMINER

★★★★

INDEPENDENT

THE CURE

By Conal Creedon   Performed by Aidan O'Hare

Mon 11 - Fri 22 April at 8:30pm
HALF MOON THEATRE
Tickets: €21
Preview Night - Mon 11 Apr: €15*
Tel. (021)4270022* or www.corkoperahouse.ie*
*Limited Early Bird €15 Tickets Available | *Booking fee may apply

WHEN I WAS GOD

BY

CÓNAL CREEDON

WHEN I WAS GOD

by
Cónal Creedon

WHEN I WAS GOD – It's the Cup Final day. Referee, Dinny Keegan is retiring from the game. The narrative is explored through the troubled mind of a league of Ireland soccer referee. Dinny has reached the pinnacle of his career – referee at the Cup Final. Alone in his dressing room his mind revisits the pivotal moment in his life that set him on the career path to become a referee.

What happens when two tribes clash under one roof? As a child, Dinny was a pawn in the battles created in the void of his parents' inability to communicate. This father/son relationship holds up a mirror to the relationship that has existed between the Gaelic game of hurling and the foreign 'Barrack game' of soccer. Dinny's father evokes images of mythical characters such as Cú Chulainn and historical martyrs such as Terence MacSwiney, who died on hunger strike in 1920 during the Irish War of Independence, in an attempt to convince young Dinny of the importance of Gaelic games and his Irish heritage.

What is the mind-set of a soccer referee? Obviously a man who loves the game and has devoted his life to it. A man who laces up his boots week after week and yet never gets to kick the ball. A man who can't jump with joy when he sees a goal being scored, a man who can't be seen to show a preference for one team over another as it would compromise his position as an impartial observer.

At half-time the spotlight shines directly down on Dinny Keegan's decision-making capability, when the ghosts of his past [his domineering father and ambitious mother] visit him in the dressing room. On the field of dreams the referee is God, but what happens when God is made man?

plays upstairs presents an american premier of WHEN I WAS GOD by award winning playwright CONAL CREEDON

directed by Tim Ruddy

featuring Gary Gregg and Michael Mellamphy

An Ingenious script....
They'll love it.
It's impossible not to.
—The Sunday Times.

Convincing and
memorably skillfull.
When I Was God
is both a treat
and a treasure.
—The Irish Times

1ST IRISH 2008

SEPTEMBER 8, 9, 14, 16, 21, 22
MANHATTAN THEATRE SOURCE
177 MacDougal St • All shows 7:30pm

Plays Upstairs presents
WHEN I WAS GOD
By Conal Creedon
Featuring Gary Gregg and Michael Mellamphy
Directed by Tim Ruddy

It's soccer cup final day. Referee Dino Keegan is retiring from

WHEN I WAS GOD

Cast : Two male actors.
One actor aged early 30s will play three parts: DINNY as a young boy, and the adult REFEREE. The actor will also play the part of young Dinny Keegan's MOTHER.
The second actor aged early 50s will play two parts. He will play the FATHER of young Dinny Keegan. He will also play the part of the sports COMMENTATOR.

Set: One raised plinth.
The set should be minimalistic. Suggestion: one raised plinth. The spirit of the dead FATHER and the COMMENTATOR are situated on this raised area, removed from the main action and giving the impression of looking down judgementally on the REFEREE & young DINNY.

Note: The driving image behind this play is that of the spirit of a dead FATHER towering over his now adult son, always lurking in the background - undermining, dismissive and negative. It is an image that is carried into the play, particularly in the context of the REFEREE [Dinny Keegan] as a boy, in his relationship with his domineering FATHER. Likewise the COMMENTATOR mirrors the father's detachment, always looking down, analysing, scrutinising. The rhythms within the play are evocative of a time when as a young boy, DINNY was sad and isolated in his bedroom listening to his mother and father fighting down stairs in the kitchen. These rhythms are carried into the present, as REFEREE finds himself once again isolated within the confines of his dressing room at half-time during the FAI Cup final.

I

[SFX: Crowd at a football match.]

[Notes:
Play opens with – REFEREE centre stage reacting to the sound of the crowd. A visual–narrative unfolds through mime/movement as REFEREE undertakes a series of official but stylised movements from the official referee's handbook.
This mime/movement should express REFEREE's personality. Controlling /Arrogant.

COMMENTATOR appears on stage – on elevated plinth behind the REFEREE. COMMENTATOR begins his match commentary. His delivery is slow, considered and deliberate.
REFEREE is centre stage. He blows his whistle, reacts and uses appropriate exaggerated hand movements to identify unfolding events on the pitch, as highlighted by the COMMENTATOR.

REFEREE's movements are co-ordinated in stylised choreography to reflect the logic of the COMMENTATOR's commentary.
Choreography: The sound of the crowd, the COMMENTATOR's commentary and the REFEREE's actions/movement should all work together as an expression of REFEREE's controlling character and spiralling frustration – in tandem with events unfolding on the pitch.

REFEREE centre stage reacts to the sound of the crowd. A visual–narrative unfolds through mime/movement as REFEREE undertakes a series of official but stylised movements from the official referee's handbook.
This mime/movement should express REFEREE's personality. Controlling /Arrogant.]

COMMENTATOR:
    Keeper places the ball on the edge of the box for a goal kick.

And with thirty-three minutes on the clock,
of this, what can only be described as
a drab and lifeless FAI Cup Final.

A clash with so much promise,
has degenerated into a scrappy game overall.
Both sides slow settling.

A long ball down the centre of the field.
Picked up by Hawkins.
Hawkins?
Hawkins to Cahill.
Cahill tries to push it through to Crowe.
Intercepted by Murray for City.
Murray plays it to Devine.
And Devine clears the ball back down the field.

[sudden burst of excitement]
Kearney running in …

REFEREE:
　　[REFEREE's hand signals are very defined and precise]
　　[react, whistle & hand movement [offside, free out]

COMMENTATOR:
　　Ooh! And it's offside.

REFEREE:
　　[react, whistle & hand movement [free out]

COMMENTATOR:
　　Quickly taken by Hawkins.
　　Intercepted by O'Brien.
　　City on the attack.

[once again a burst of excitement]
Once again Kearney on the ball…
Ouuaah!

REFEREE:

[react, whistle & hand movement [foul]

COMMENTATOR:

And O'Brien literally pushed off the ball and over the sideline.
Hawkins's running in.
A bit of argy-bargy going on down there –
between O'Brien and the big Shelburne defender …

REFEREE: *[attempts to keep control]*
[react, whistle & hand movement [free out]
Whistle-Whistle!

COMMENTATOR:

Referee Dino Keegan taking control …
… having a few words with Hawkins and O'Brien.

REFEREE:

Whistle!

COMMENTATOR:

Free quickly taken. He sends it high.
John O' Flynn's on the ball …

[SFX: crowd roar as if reacting to foul on the field]

COMMENTATOR:

Oaahh! And O' Flynn's been taken down!
Full view of Referee Dino Keegan.

REFEREE:

> *[centre stage under spotlight]*
> *[sharp whistle, severe actions indicate free]*
> Player! Player! I'm on to you! I'm on to you!
> You pull another stunt like that –
> No! Don't even think about it.
> You mess with me, you're off the field!
>
> And you! *[calling another player to order]*
> Yeah, you!
> *[calls him back using his finger, expressing control]*
> Tuck in your shirt!

COMMENTATOR:

> …and the seconds are ticking down in this, the first half of
> the FAI Cup Final. Referee Dino Keegan once again checking
> his watch.

REFEREE:

> Now! *[blows whistle]* – Play ball!

[SFX: roar of crowd]

COMMENTATOR:

> Oooaah! A blistering rocket just two inches over the cross bar.
> A missed opportunity for city. A missed chance to break the
> deadlock.

REFEREE:

> *[REFEREE looks at watch and blows whistle for end of half]*

COMMENTATOR:

> And, there it is, the half time whistle.
> And as the two teams leave the field, the score is still nil-all.
> In this, what can only be described as a sloppy first half.

No doubt there'll be some stiff words from both managers in
the dressing room.
Of course – special mention today for the man in the middle.
Referee Dino Keegan, who is retiring from the game.
Hanging up his whistle – so to speak.
A man who has devoted much of his life to the sport of soccer.

[SFX: fade crowd]

[Transition: COMMENTATOR on the elevated plinth behind the REFEREE.
Transition – COMMENTATOR becomes the spirit of Referee's dead father
[FATHER]
The spirit of FATHER does not interact with REFEREE, although the
REFEREE shouts directly in his direction as if talking into space.]

REFEREE: [addressing the spirit of his dead FATHER]
    D'ya see that, Dad! D'ya see that!

FATHER:
[FATHER does not engage with the REFEREE. He stands there barking
out orders looking directly at the audience not reacting to REFEREE]
    Pull on it, man!

REFEREE:
    Out there, I'm the man!
    The main man!
    25 years out there.
    Still on the ball.
    Keepin' up with play. Keeping up with play.

FATHER: [barks out order]
    He will!

REFEREE:
    I've served my time, Dad.

I've served my time.
D'ya hear me!
Out there, there's no messin' with me.
They listen to me, or they're off the field!

FATHER:
He bloody well will!

REFEREE:
There's no messin' with me, Dad!

FATHER:
He will! I said! He will!

REFEREE:
I've served my time, Dad!

FATHER:
He'll serve his time, Missus.
I'm tellin' ya now.
He will!

[Transition: – REFEREE to MOTHER

REFEREE becomes MOTHER, just by the very fact that he begins addressing the FATHER directly and the FATHER addresses him/her. REFEREE to MOTHER transition does not require props or a falsetto voice as this might develop into pantomime maybe a simple hand gesture of folding arms.]

[Note: Establish a rhythm in the dialog between FATHER and MOTHER – rhythm that sounds like the rhythm of a game of table tennis.]

MOTHER:
He won't!

FATHER:

He will!

MOTHER:

He won't!

FATHER:

He will!

MOTHER:

He won't!

FATHER:

He will!

MOTHER:

He won't!

FATHER:

He will!

MOTHER:

Well I said he won't!

FATHER:

Oh, yeah? Well I said he will!

MOTHER:

And I said he won't …

FATHER:

He will!

MOTHER:

He won't!

FATHER:

>He will!

MOTHER:

>D'ya know what's wrong with you!
>D'ya hear me?
>I said, d'ya know what's wrong with you!

FATHER:

>Me, Missus?

MOTHER:

>You thinks, you knows everything!

FATHER:

>Sur' Jesus! look at yourself, Missus!

MOTHER:

>What about me?

FATHER:

>You thinks you're always right!

MOTHER:

>I thinks I'm always right?
>I knows I'm always right!

FATHER:

>You knows yer always right?

MOTHER:

>Sur' you knows everything!

FATHER:

>And, you're always right?

MOTHER:
> You knows everything!

FATHER:
> You're always right!

MOTHER:
> Knows everything!

FATHER:
> Always right!

MOTHER:
> Knows everything!

FATHER:
> Always right!

MOTHER:
> Knows everything!

FATHER: *[shout]*
> You're always Right!

MOTHER:
[Speaking to the unseen young son DINNY – Clearly DINNY isn't there but MOTHER gestures as if she's speaking to a child.]
> Dinny boy?
> You go up to bed there like a good young fella.
> Meself an' yer fadder has a few things to sort out.

[Speaking to FATHER]
> Now, he's going to college,
> and no more about it!

FATHER:

> He will not!

MOTHER:

> I said he will!

FATHER:

> Well, I said he won't!

MOTHER:

> And I said he will!

FATHER:

> He won't!

MOTHER:

> He will!

FATHER:

> Listen now, Missus!
> He'll serve his time.
> He'll serve his time, alright!
> He'll hold a trade.
> He will! He'll hold a trade like me and me fadder.
> D'ya hear me!
> I'm tellin' ya now, Missus – he'll serve his time!

MOTHER:

> He will not!

FATHER:

> He will!

MOTHER:

> He won't!

FATHER:

He will!

MOTHER:

Look it?
I know what you want!
You want my child to have dirt under his fingernails,
muck behind his ears.
Shit for brains...

FATHER:

Shit for brains?

MOTHER:

Shit for brains, like you!

FATHER:

Me?
Shit for brains?

Jesus, look into yer own head, Missus, what do you see?
What do you want!

I'll tell ya what ya want, Missus.
You want a doc – tor!
That's what you want.
You want a doctor, a dentist, a lawyer.

You want to tell de street, dat's my son.
Dat's my son the doctor!
All a' ye tip yer hats! On yer knees! To the doc-tor.
My son! The doctor!
That's what you want!

[whisper] But do ya know what you'll get, Missus?

You'll get a son alright!
A son, a doc – tor.
A son, that's embarrassed by you!
He'll be embarrassed by the dirt a' yer hair
and the words…
The words you'll never understand….

Sshhhhit for brains, me!?
Don't make me laugh…
Look int've yer own brain Missus – what do ya see?
Look int've yer own brain Missus – and ask yourself,
what do you want?

MOTHER:
What I want?
What I want!
What I want – is what I don't want!
'cause what I don't want,
is another you!

FATHER:
Another me?
Jesus, all I'm sayin' is – he'll serve his time.

MOTHER:
And all I'm sayin' is – he won't!

FATHER:
He will!

MOTHER:
He won't!

FATHER:
He will!

MOTHER:
He won't!

FATHER:
He will!

MOTHER:
He won't!

FATHER:
He will!

[Transition – MOTHER gradually becomes REFEREE. He's lying down on the bench]

MOTHER:
He won't!

FATHER:
He will!

MOTHER / REFEREE: *[Transition]*
He won't!

FATHER:
He will!

MOTHER / REFEREE: *[Transition]*
He won't!

FATHER:
He will!

[Transition: MOTHER to REFEREE: In the transition from MOTHER to REFEREE his response becomes more passive, matter-of-fact and

emotionally removed – the transition also involves the FATHER becoming a spirit again – in effect FATHER and REFEREE do not interact with each other – but rather speak directly to audience]

REFEREE:
He won't!

FATHER:
He will!

REFEREE:
He won't!

FATHER:
He will!

REFEREE:
And I'm up in bed,

FATHER: *[directly at audience]*
He will!

REFEREE:
Listenin' and thinking,

FATHER:
He will!

REFEREE:
Listenin' an' thinkin',
night after night.

FATHER:
Always right! Always right!

REFEREE:

    After-night! After-night!

FATHER: *[mood changes to seductive]*

    In close,

REFEREE: *[masturbation implied, echoing the previous rhythm]*

    And me?

FATHER:

    In close, Dinny boy.

REFEREE:

    I'm the Hand King!

FATHER:

    Pull on it, man!

REFEREE:

    I'm the Hand King, yanking!

FATHER:

    Gowan, Dinny boy!

REFEREE:

    Breathtakin'!

FATHER: *[once again building in anger]*

    Pull on it!

REFEREE:

    Heartbreaking!

FATHER:

    Pull on it, man!

REFEREE:

    Love-making,

FATHER:

    Pull on it, man!

REFEREE:

    – to me!

FATHER & REFEREE:

    Pull! Pull! Pull on the fuckin' thing!

[SFX: crowd roar]

[Transition: – REFEREE to DINNY
When FATHER is speaking to MOTHER, we don't actually see her on stage. FATHER is talking to MOTHER about DINNY.
DINNY is standing there looking – realising that he is a pawn in a bigger battle.]

FATHER:

    Now, Missus?
    Let de boy,
    Let the boy speak for himself.
    Dinny, I'll ask ya the once and the once only!
    You tell yer Mam,
    What do you wanna be when you grows up, Son?

DINNY:

    [Surprised – for once he's asked his opinion]
    Me, Dad?
    Yer askin' me?

FATHER:

    Come on now …

Look her int've her eyes, Son.
Look her int've her eyes. An' tell her straight.
Tell her straight to her face…

DINNY:

What do I want to be?

FATHER:

There's no use tellin' me, Son.
Talk to yer mother.

DINNY:

Eh, Mam, When I grows up…
When I grows up,
I wants to be a,
I wants to be a
… a soccer player.

FATHER: *[furious]*

A what!

DINNY: *[unsure]*

Ah soccer player, Dad?

FATHER:

Soccer player! Soccer player!
Jesus Christ, Dinny boy,
you can't play soccer for a livin'!
Like who's gonna feed yer wife an' childer'?

DINNY:

Wife an' childer', Dad?

FATHER:

Who's gonna feed 'em!?

DINNY:

But I'm only ten …

FATHER:

Jesus, in my day a lad your age,
be earnin' a man's wage,
at this stage!
Sure you're gonna have a wife and childer some day? Aren't ya!

DINNY: *[Helpless look of indecision]*

Mam?

FATHER:

But you're gonna get married someday?
Well aren't ya, Son?
Aren't ya!

DINNY:

Eh, I don't know, Dad!

FATHER:

[mocking] I don't know, Dad?

Yer dammed right you don't know!
How could you know.…
When all ye want is to do is play that namby-pamby's game,
Hah?!
A-a-a a foreign game! Hah!
Over my dead body, boy!
Over my dead body! D'ya hear me!

[to MOTHER]
I'm tellin' you now, Missus!
eight–hundred years of oppression, by them imperialist
bastards,

and my own flesh and blood –
my own flesh and blood have the gall
to be tellin' me straight to my face
that he wants to be a soccer player!

A soccer player …
Well that's some how d'ya do, all the same, hah?!

Hurlin'! Son!
Hurlin'!
That's the game for you, boy!
Hurlin'! A man's game.

Take that look off yer face right quick now!
Hurlin' was good enough for Cú Chulainn,
it's good enough for you, boy!

DINNY:

But my friends!

FATHER:

Don't mind your friends!
Sure, Jesus, if your friends all went out and jumped in to the river,
I suppose you'd jump in after 'em, would ya!
Well, would you?!
[Roars] Would You!

DINNY:

Eh, I dunno, Dad…

FATHER:

[Mocking] I dunno, Dad!

Where were your friends?

Where were your friends when Patrick Pearse
and the boys of the 1916 rising were boarded up in the GPO?
Hah!

DINNY:

1916, Dad?

FATHER:

Where were they!? Where were they!?

DINNY:

They were, eh?

FATHER:

I'll tell ya where they were, boy!
They were out playin' soccer! That's where they were.
You'll play hurlin'.
You'll play hurlin' and enjoy it!
You'll play hurlin' and enjoy it! And no more about it!

[Transition – DINNY to REFEREE]
[REFEREE – Pause for a moment as if watching the memory of FATHER
fade. He then turns and addresses the audience directly]

REFEREE:

And, I played hurling alright.
Up the old Mon field after school.
Thirty wild boys – chasing a sliotar.
And me dad on the ditch …

FATHER:

Pull on it, man! Pull on it!

REFEREE:

I played hurlin' alright,
an' me dad on the ditch …

FATHER: *[manic]*
>Pull on de bloody' thing, Dinny boy will ya!

REFEREE: *[Whispers, then stands back and looks at the memory of his FATHER]*
>And me dad on the ditch …

FATHER:
>Jesus Christ!
>Hook de ball! D'ye hear me!
>Attack, boy! Attack!
>God almighty, pull on it, man!
>Shorten yer stick!
>Get in hard! In hard, boy! Get in close! In close! And …
>Pull on the fuckin' ball will ya, Dinny boy!

REFEREE:
>And me dad on the ditch….

[Transition – REFEREE to DINNY]

FATHER: *[rising in tension]*
>Get up for it, Dinny boy! Get up for it!

[FATHER gets excited as DINNY makes a heroic run up the field and scores a point. FATHER's delivery is highly animated – while DINNY mimes the action – He rises to catch a high ball – then miming as if running the length of the field with his outstretched arm balancing the ball on the tip of his hurley.
DINNY's movement is in slow motion/strobe, moving like a ballerina, weaving in and out between his vicious opponents – swerving, ducking and diving.
Eventually he hits the ball and scores an incredible point.]

FATHER:

> You have him, you have him!
> Gowan, Dinny boy!
> Keep goin'! Keep goin'!
> [reaction] Oh, Jeeezus! Now, Dinny boy! Now!
> Release it! Release it!
> Now, Dinny boy! Now!
> Hit the fuckin' ball, will ya, Dinny boy!

[SFX : crowd roar as DINNY hits the ball]
[FATHER watches as the ball goes over the bar for a point.
We see the delight in FATHER's and DINNY's faces]

FATHER:

> Yes!
> Great point, Dinny boy! Great point!

[DINNY over-reacts in the fashion of a soccer player and pulls his jersey
over his head. As DINNY peacocks around the stage FATHER's delight
turns from dismay to disgust.]

FATHER: [angry]

> Hey! Hey! Hey!
> What the hell are ya at, Dinny boy!
> Pull down your jersey will ya! For Christ's sake!
> Your like an aul' doll!
> [hissed] Jesus Christ …

[DINNY pulls his jersey from his head and the delight turns to
disappointment in both DINNY and FATHER]

FATHER:

> For God's sake, Dinny boy!
> Would ya ever grow up and cop on to yourself!

REFEREE: *[to audience]*
  And me Dad on the ditch, me Dad on the ditch …

* * *

[After match, FATHER talks to DINNY]

FATHER:
  Dinny?

  You played well today, Son. Ya played well …
  Now –
  I'm not taking away from that great point you got.
  But there's 60 minutes of blood, sweat and tears out there.
  A game isn't won by a flash in the pan.
  You must keep takin' your points …

  A bad point is as important as a good point.
  Do you know what I'm sayin'?
  It's all about focus, Son. 60 minutes of focus …

  See, I don't think you're listening to me.
  You must keep yer eye –
  D'ya hear me? You must keep yer eye always –
  always on the ball.
  Say it back to me?

DINNY:
  I must keep me eye on the ball.

FATHER:
  No, Son, No!
  Always! Always!
  You must keep yer eye always on the ball!

DINNY:

    I must keep my eye always on the ball?

FATHER:

    That's right!
    You must keep your eye always on the ball.
    Even – listen to me now.
    Even when the ball isn't there at all.
    D'ya hear me?
    You must keep your eye always on the ball,
    even when the ball isn't there at all …

[DINNY is preoccupied with his finger - hurt during the game]
[DINNY raises up his finger]

FATHER:

    What? What!
    Don't mind your finger!

DINNY:

    That big fella nearly broke me hand, Dad.

FATHER:

    Here show us?
    Naw, Naw, that's only a scratch!

DINNY:

    Scratch, Dad?

FATHER:

    It looks worse than it is, Son.
    See, it only looks big 'cause your hands are so small!
    That's all!

    'Tis all part of the game, Dinny boy.

'Tis kill or be killed out there.
Survival of the fittest.

Big fish eat small fish – and small fish are bait.
That's the first thing you gotta learn!

And anyone who'll tell you that it don't matter if you win or
lose,
That it's all about how you play the game …
Well they are talking through their hole, Son!
It's all about winnin' – always about winnin'!
Is now, was then and ever shall be about winnin'!

See, the day you win the Harty Cup is gonna be the greatest
day of my life.
'Cause that day pinned on your chest will be the Harty medal.
It's a badge of honour, Son.
Pinned on yer chest, like a suit of armour protecting your
heart.
And that medal not only tells to the world that you're a
winner, Son.
No, no, no …
That medal not only tells to the world that you're a team
player.
No, no, no …
That medal tells the world that of all the men in all this city –
you were hand picked to play your part in a great historic
victory.

That medal is all about the three R-s, Son!
Recognition, Redemption and Retribution.
Redemption for all the cold and wet and dark winter evenings
walking home from the Mon field.
Recognition, for all the black and blue bruises and broken
bones.

And Retribution, for all the pain of defeat, despair and
disappointment you'll meet along the way.

I'll tell you one thing about a Harty medal, Son.
Right through your life, no matter how low things go,
you'll always be held with – respect – as a man who won the
Harty Cup.
I've known men give up their friends,
give up their family,
even give up their religion –
but in all my life I've never known a man to give up his Harty
Cup medal – never!
They'll carry it to the grave – with 'um.

And in a hundred years from now –
When me and you are long dead, Son.
There'll be a builder's labourer clearing out an old house.
And there, in the bottom of a drawer, wrapped in an aul
hankie,
he'll come across your medal.
He will!
Dinny Keegan – Harty Cup Final.

And though he'll not know who the hell you are.
The power of that medal – will transport him right back,
down the Park.
To that glorious afternoon …
– The roar of the crowd, the clash of the ash, the blood and
bandage …

[Pause as FATHER *is brought back to the reality of the situation]*
But Jesus you gotta get in hard, boy!
In hard and pull on the fuckin' thing!
In hard!

Have ya got that int've your head, you have?
Listen to me now, there's no need worrying your Mam about
that little nick on your finger or the slap on the shins.
D'ya hear me!?
And if she asks ya?
Just look her straight int've the eyes and tell her – 'tis nothin'!

DINNY:

Tis nothin', Dad?

FATHER:

That's right, Son, 'tis nothin'.
La, we'll drop into Linehan's, for d'aul toffee apple on the way
down along, alright!?

DINNY: [receptive to bribe]

'Tis nothin', Dad! 'Tis nothin'…

FATHER: [passionately logical]

I mean Jesus, for centuries –
The men of Cork stood shoulder-to-shoulder, man-to-man
against:
the Viking, the Dane, the Saxon and the Black and Tan.
'Tis better to be carried off the battlefield
on the flat of yer back on yer shield,
than to hide or runaway.

And I tell ya now, any man who lives to fight another day
have a yella' streak the width of Patrick's street runnin' down
his back.
Sur' Jesus, didn't Terence MacSwiney say it – and he dyin' on
hunger strike:
'Tis not those who inflict the most pain – but those who can
endure the most pain – that'll win the war.

DINNY: *[attempting to calm FATHER]*
    It's okay, Dad, 'tis nothin'! 'Tis nothin' …

FATHER: *[reasoning]*
    See, do ya know where yer goin' wrong, Son!
    You must get in, Son!
    Ya must get in hard!
    Give 'um stick!
    That's where you're goin' wrong!

    Ya see – hurlin'?
    Hurlin's a one–on–one, Son!
    There's no back passin' in hurlin'.
    'Tis attackin' all the time.
    You take no prisoners in hurlin'!

    The hurley? The hurley's like an extension of the hand.
    That's what it is, 'tis an extension of yer hand.
    'Tis all, hand, eye and ball co-ordination, that's hurlin', Son.

    An' one a' these years, I'm tellin' you straight now!
    I'll be down the Park.
    And you'll be captaining the North Mon, Dinny boy!
    And I'll be lookin' up at you, liftin' de Harty Cup above your
    head.

    And I'll be lookin' up at you, Son, with tears in me eyes.
    And, and you'll be liftin' de Harty Cup above your head!
    For the North Mon, Dinny boi! That I may be struck dead!
    You will!
    For the North Mon, I'm tellin' you now!
    D'ya hear me! The Harty Cup!

    But Jesus, you must give 'em stick.
    And when it's a fifty-fifty ball, what d'ya do?
    What d'ya do?!

DINNY:

Eh? In close, Dad?

FATHER:

In close, dead right, boy!
D'ya hear me, Son …
Ya must get in close and pull!
Pull on the fuckin' thing!
In close and …

DINNY:

Pull on it!

FATHER:

That's right, Son! You pull on the fuckin' thing!

* * *

[Sudden location change – FATHER and DINNY are in sweetshop]

FATHER: *[As if talking to the shopkeeper]*
[DINNY expresses delight to what FATHER is saying]
Eh, two toffee apples there if yea have 'em, Mr. Linehan!

The young fella?
The young fella's a great little hurler! Great little hurler!
The next Christy Ring, swear to God!
That I may be struck dead now, the next Christy Ring!!
[Seductive]
Dinny boy, there's yer toffee apple there!
[bribe] And listen –
There's no need worrying yer Mam about,
those few cuts an' bruises'?
D'ya hear me? No need worrying yer mam, at all …

DINNY:

Eh? No, Dad!

FATHER: *[to shopkeeper]*

And a few bull's eyes too, while yer at it …

[DINNY is excited, reacts]

FATHER: *[dangles the sweets like a bribe]*

… An' listen?

Don't forget, now –

When yer mam asks ya about that little nick on yer finger?

Tell her, 'tis nothin'.

DINNY:

'Tis nothin', Dad!

FATHER:

That's right, 'tis nothin'!

FATHER & DINNY: *[in unison]*

In close and pull on the fuckin' thing!

* * *

[Transition – DINNY to REFEREE – REFEREE addresses the audience directly]

REFEREE:

In close and pull on the fuckin' thing?

My dad,

lived for the hurlin', lived for the hurlin'!

But I played hurlin'.
Black an' blue shins, broke me thumb, lost me teeth.
I played hurling, alright. Made a man a' me.
Made a ten year old man a' me.
Week after week, body: bruised, battered and bloody.
I played hurlin' alright…

[FATHER *roaring from the ditch.*]

FATHER:

Go on, Dinny boi! Get up fer it! Get up fer it!
Jeezus Chris…

[We see DINNY *going up for the ball –* FATHER'S *attitude changes to worry as he sees* DINNY *being hit on the head by an opposition hurley*]

DINNY: [*clutching head and roaring in pain*]
Ah, Goddy!

FATHER: [*concerned/worried*]
Here show us!

[DINNY *holding his head - obviously in pain*]

DINNY:

Ah Goddy! Ah Goddy! Ah Goddy! Ah God!

[FATHER *is concerned/worried. His worry escalates as he investigates* DINNY'S *head. Cleary* FATHER *is more concerned about* MOTHER'S *reaction to* DINNY'S *head injury – than the extent of the damage done to the boy*]

FATHER:

You're ok, Son! You're ok, Son!
There's a good lad! You're ok!

You're ok….
Here give us a look of it, Show us?
Show us? Ouuh …
Eh, yer alright
'Tis eh, 'tis more blood than anythin', Son …
Look, eh, I'll eh, I'll bring ya down to The North Infirmary Hospital
on the way home.
Get the doctor to take a look of it.
The head's a delicate thing.
Come on, Dinny boy! Come on!
We'll cut down by the chicken chokers and across the top a' Gurranabraher.
Get the doctor to take a look of it …
Honestly now Son, 'tis nothin'.
You just got a bit of a fright that's all.
That's all.
Looks worse than what it is.
[obviously very worried]
Come on Dinny boy, Come on!

∗ ∗ ∗

[Sudden scene change.
They are leaving the hospital - obviously the FATHER is relieved. DINNY is dazed after the ordeal]

FATHER: *[relieved – attitude change – lionised again]*
Here?
Show us?
Six stitches! I mean six stitches is nothin' for a young fella!
But, the aul' head's a delicate thing.
You'd want to be careful with the aul' head all the same …

DINNY:

    I could always get a helmet, Dad!

FATHER:

    A helmet? A helmet!
    Sur' Christy Ring never wore a helmet!
    You'll be fine boy. You'll be better before yer married.

    Now when ya gets in home, the best thing for you to do,
    is to go straight up the stairs to bed.
    D'ya hear me?
    Dere's no need worrying yer mam about that cut on yer head.

DINNY:

    'Tis nothin', Dad?

FATHER:

    That's right! 'Tis nothin'!

[Transition – DINNY to MOTHER – as FATHER and DINNY arrive into house]

FATHER: [as if sneaking into the house - hushed tones]
    Dinny boy, go on up them stairs, I'll bring ya up your tea in a minute …

[Transition – DINNY to MOTHER]

MOTHER: [MOTHER as if clutching DINNY's head]
    Child of grace!

FATHER:

    Huh? [or look of guilt]

MOTHER: *[inspecting DINNY's head]*
    Mother of God!

FATHER:
    Go on Dinny! Go on!

MOTHER:
    What in the name of!

FATHER:
    Eh, 'tis eh, 'tis eh?

MOTHER:
    Jesus Christ and his Holy Mother!

FATHER: *[attempts to walk away]*
    'Tis nothin'…

MOTHER:
    'Tis nothin'? 'Tis nothin'!
    Yoouuu!

FATHER:
    Who me?

MOTHER:
    Yeah, you! Come over here! Come over here, you!
    Did ya see de state of that child's head!

FATHER:
    No! No honestly now, Missus,
    Brother Keenan took a look of it…

MOTHER:
    Br. Keenan, took a look of it? Tuck-a-luk-av-it!

FATHER:

    … said 'twas nothing.

MOTHER:

    … 'twas nothin'?

FATHER:

    Ehh? 'Twas was a high ball comin' in…

MOTHER:

    High ball? High-ball!
    High-ball me eye-ball!
    That does it!
    Never again! You mark my words!
    Ne-ver-a-gain!
    If I as much as see that child with a hurley in his hand,
    I swear, I swear to Christ….

FATHER:

    Sur' Jesus, if he stayed in close, like I told him!

    [Speaking to DINNY]
    I mean,
    how many times have I told ya!
    Stick in close, boy! Stick in close!
    But sure Jesus, I may as well be talkin' to the wall.

MOTHER:

    There's no child a' mine – comin' home here, week after week,
    mutilated by a bunch a yahoos – with sticks!
    A-a-and all in the name of sport!
    Jesus Christ, you should know better!
    That leg a' yours …

[MOTHER points at FATHER's bad leg – limp]

FATHER:

Don't start, Missus! Don't start!

MOTHER:

'Twas hurlin' made shit of yer shin!
'Twas hurlin' made a cripple out of you!

FATHER:

I wear this limp with pride, Missus!

MOTHER:

Pride?

FATHER:

'Tis a man's game!
'T'll toughen the lad up!

MOTHER:

Toughen him up?
'T'll break every bone in his body!
Mother of God!
Never again! Never again!
If you left the poor child play soccer like he wanted …

FATHER:

Soccer?!
[cold]
Hold it there now, Missus!
I always given into you on the rulin' and the schoolin' of this
young fella.
But I'm makin' me stand on the soccer!
As long as I live …
there'll be no son a mine ever gonna play that shaggin' game!
Not now! Not ever! Never!

MOTHER:

> Well, he's not playin' hurlin'!

FATHER:

> He will!

MOTHER:

> He won't!

FATHER:

> He will!

MOTHER:

> He won't!

FATHER:

> He will!

MOTHER:

> He won't!

[Transition – MOTHER gradually reverts to being the REFEREE]

FATHER:

> He will!

REFEREE:

> He won't.

[REFEREE and FATHER looking directly out addressing the audience]

FATHER:

> He will!

REFEREE:
>   Listening.

FATHER:
>   He will!

REFEREE:
>   To the ...

FATHER:
>   He will!

REFEREE:
>   same aul',

FATHER:
>   He will!

REFEREE:
>   down stairs,

FATHER:
>   He will!

[REFEREE – over next series of interactions with FATHER – REFEREE gradually moves to reclining position on plinth as if going to bed as a young boy - DINNY]

REFEREE:
>   same aul',

FATHER:
>   He will!

REFEREE:

ding-dong!

FATHER:

He will!

REFEREE:

Same aul',

FATHER:

He will!

REFEREE:

ping pong!

FATHER:

He will!

REFEREE:

Same aul',

FATHER:

He will!

REFEREE:

chit-chat!

FATHER:

He will!

REFEREE:

Always right! Always right!

FATHER:

He will!

REFEREE:
  Night after night!

FATHER:
  He will!

REFEREE:
  And I'm the Hand King!

FATHER: *[whisper seductive]*
  In close…

REFEREE:
  The Hand King – Yanking!

FATHER:
  In close, boy!

REFEREE:
  Breath-taking.

FATHER:
  Get in close!

REFEREE:
  Heartbreaking.

FATHER:
  Ya must get in close!

REFEREE:
  Love–making.

FATHER:
  Ya must get in close, Dinny boy!

REFEREE:
    Love making to me!

FATHER & REFEREE: *[shout]*
    Pull! Pull on the fuckin' thing!

[SFX: of crowd roar]

[Transition – REFEREE to DINNY – next morning – DINNY is in bed asleep]

FATHER:
    Mornin', Son?

DINNY: *[wakes up suddenly]*
    Dad?!

FATHER:
    Your mother and me have decided that from now on …
    You're gonna play …
    You're gonna play …
    Look! Your mother and me have decided,
    that from now on …
    yer gonna play…
    Table tennis …

DINNY: *[confused]*
    Table tennis?

FATHER:
    Now!
    Now I explained t've her,
    is table tennis any game for a man to be playin'?!
    Well is it! Hah?!

DINNY: *[unsure]*
> Eh, it is, Dad?

FATHER:
> What!

DINNY:
> Eh, it's not, Dad!

FATHER:
> Yer dammed right 'tis not!
> Table tennis?

[Transition – DINNY to REFEREE]
[FATHER's continuing rant is overlapped by the REFEREE's observations]

REFEREE: *[overlap]*
> One thing about me mam. She was always right!

FATHER:
> I mean what sort of a game is table tennis?

REFEREE:
> No! Two things about me mam. She was always right …

FATHER:
> Jesus, 'tis only the girls an' the Chineeee plays table tennis!

REFEREE:
> …and at the end a' the day…

FATHER:
> Grunt!

REFEREE:

> My mam, always won over my dad…
> and table tennis was the game.

[FATHER *speaks in grunts – but the logic of his words is echoed in the rhythm and the placing of the grunts.*]

FATHER:

> A namby-pamby's grunt is table grunt.

REFEREE:

> And I played table tennis!

FATHER:

> I tell ya now.
> I grunt ya straight!
> I'd boil me head in Parazone,
> before any grunt of mine be playin' dat namby-pamby's grunt!
> That's what I grunt.
> Grunt me head in grunt-azone!
> Grunt!
> I would!
> Grunt!

REFEREE:

> I played table tennis alright!
> Every Wednesday after school, the Mon Primary Hall.
> And I was handy.
> Two whole years lookin' over the net – flaking a white paper ball.
> Table tennis trophies and medals – piling up on top a' the telly.
> Two whole years. And me dad?
> Me dad only talked to me in grunts.

FATHER: *[as if calling DINNY]*
    Grunt!
    Grunt!

[Transition – REFEREE to DINNY]
[Conversation between FATHER and DINNY: the logic of FATHER's words is echoed in his grunts]

FATHER:
    Grunt?!

Dinny: *[confused as the FATHER seems to be calling him]*

FATHER:
    Grunt?

DINNY:
    Ya want something from the shop, Dad!

FATHER:
    Grunt!   *[yes]*

FATHER:
    A grunt of grunts!   *[a pack of fags]*

DINNY:
    Ten or twenty, Dad?

FATHER:
    Grunt-y!   *[twenty]*

DINNY:
    Do ya need matches?

FATHER:
    Grunt-grunt!   *[I don't]*

[Transition – DINNY to REFEREE]

REFEREE:
    Two years, he's sittin' there, staring at the black and white
    screen.
    Dazzled by my table tennis trophies on top of the telly.
    Never opening his mouth except for the odd …

FATHER:
    Grunt!

REFEREE:
    Never sayin' a word.
    Two whole years!
    Just sittin' there sayin' nothin' but the odd …

FATHER:
    Grunt?

[Transition: REFEREE to DINNY]

FATHER: *[tone changes slightly more friendly]*
    Grunt?

*[DINNY looks to FATHER confused – it takes a few attempts before
DINNY understands the grunts]*

FATHER:
    Grunt?
    Yer grunt was gruntin' – you've a big grunt on Grunt-urday.

DINNY: *[confused]*
    Huh? [or look]

FATHER:

I grunt,
grunt mother grunt sayin' – you've a big grunt on Saturday!

DINNY:

What's that, Dad?

FATHER: *[louder]*

I grunt, yer mother was gruntin' you've a big game on Grunt-urday!

DINNY:

The Schools Championships Final, Dad?

FATHER:

The Grunts Championships Final.

DINNY:

That's right, Dad! Up in the Parochial Hall.

FATHER:

The Parochial grunt?

DINNY:

I'm captaining the North Mon,

[A visible change comes over FATHER's face as he hears the words North Mon]

FATHER: *[whispers to himself]*

The Mon? The Mon?
Yer playin' for the North Mon, Dinny boy?!

DINNY:

I'm playin' a fella from, St. Coleman's Fermoy, Dad …

FATHER: *[disbelief]*
> The Mon playin' St. Coleman's?

DINNY:
> School's Championship Final, Dad …

FATHER:
> Like a class of a – Harty Cup Final? Is it?

DINNY:
> The Harty Cup, Dad?

[DINNY realises this might be a way back into FATHER's life]

> Eh? Sorta' like the Harty Cup, – now that you mention it.
> 'Cept, it's not hurlin', like.
> It's table tennis, like.

FATHER: *[thinking to himself like a dream]*
> The North Mon and St. Coleman's?
> The Mon and Coleman's …
> An' d'ya think you'll win, Son?

DINNY:
> Do I think I'll win, Dad?
> Do I think I'll win?

[Transition – DINNY to REFEREE]

REFEREE:
> I could see that glint in his eyes.
> I could hear his brain ticking.
> It was like all the hurling greats were filing by two by two:
> Christy Ring, Paddy Barry, Jack Lynch, Jimmy Barry Murphy
> …

FATHER:

Sorta' like a Harty Cup Final, you say?
So tell us? What's this table tennis malarkey all about anyhow?

[Transition – REFEREE to DINNY]
[DINNY realises this is his chance to become close to FATHER again –
so he draws on hurling comparisons that were previously expressed by
FATHER]

DINNY:

Table tennis, Dad? Table tennis?
Well it's a one on one, Dad, y' know.
Two players, two bats and a ball.
It's fast. Very fast …

FATHER: [defensive]

As fast as hurlin', Son?

DINNY: [attempting to draw the FATHER in]

Ah sur' hurlin' the fastest game in de world, Dad.
Everyone know that.
But de table tennis?
Table tennis would come in a close second …

FATHER:

A close second you say?

DINNY:

Chalk it down, Dad.
It's kill or be killed out there …

FATHER:

Kill or be killed!?

DINNY:

Big fish eat small fish –

FATHER:

Big fish eat small fish?

[Remembering FATHER's words – DINNY repeats his hurling analogy back to FATHER in an attempt to draw him in]

DINNY:

That's right, Dad…
And small fish are only bait!
See, table tennis is all down to reaction…
The bat? The bat's like, eh?
Well, the bat's like an extension a' the hand, d'ya know!
It's all about hand, eye and ball coordination.

FATHER:

Hand, eye and ball coordination?

DINNY:

That's right, Dad!
It's attacking all the time.
There's no back–passing in table tennis, Dad …

FATHER:

Jesus?

DINNY:

Ya take no prisoners in table tennis.

FATHER:

Gowan?

DINNY:

And it don't matter how you play the game –
It's all about winnin'!
Is now, was then and ever shall be – all about winnin'.
Winner takes all, Dad …
A table tennis medal is something ya take to yer grave …

FATHER:

Really?

DINNY:

It's all about the three Rs, Dad!

FATHER:

The three Rs you say …

DINNY:

Redemption, recognition …
And eh? And eh? And eh …

FATHER:

Retribution, Son?

DINNY:

Retribution! That's right Dad!

FATHER:

Jesus, The aul' table tennis don't sound a million miles away
from the aul' hurling, all the same now, do it?

DINNY:

An' d'ya know?
Ya must always keep yer eye on the ball, Dad.
Even when the ball isn't there at all!

FATHER:

> And the final's on Sat-ur-day you say?

DINNY:

> Up Parochial Hall!

FATHER:

> And are you trainin', Son?

DINNY:

> Doin' a bit!

FATHER: *[shouts to unseen MOTHER]*

> Hoi! Missus!
> Clear off de table there, will ya.
> Meself and Dinny are talkin' tactics.

[FATHER draws DINNY close to him and gives him sporting advice]

FATHER:

> Listen to me now, Son.
> When you're up there on Saturday,
> an' you're facin' yer man from St Coleman's.
> Look him straight int've the eyes.
> Make him feel small!
> D'ya hear me! You must make him feel small.
> And when you makes him feel small,
> just watch him – shrink away in front a' your eyes – to nothing
> at all.
> Then!
> Then ya must get in hard, Son! In hard!
> D'ya hear me!
> In hard and pull on the fuckin' thing!

* * *

[Scene Change – School's Championship final]

DINNY:

    Saturday morning. Parochial hall.
    The School's Championship final.
    Me against St. Coleman's – two games all!

FATHER:

    No fault, Dinny boy!

DINNY:

    Threw away the first game.
    Slow settling.
    Poxed in the second game: 23-21.

FATHER:

    Gowan Dinny, you can take him!

[DINNY moves as if playing table tennis. FATHER shouting encouragement]

DINNY:

    But I came back!
    Dish! Dish! Dish!

FATHER:

    My boy, Dinny boy!

DINNY:

    21-15 to the Mon!

FATHER:

    Gowan, Dinny boy!

DINNY:

>And I came back.
>Dish! Dish! Dish!
>21-13,

FATHER:

>Doubt ya, Dinny boy!

DINNY:

>On a roll! Two games all!
>Best of five!
>The decider ...

FATHER:

>I'm with ya Dinny boy! I'm with ya ...

DINNY:

>And I'm staring this fella from St. Coleman's straight into the
>eyes,
>and he's getting' smaller and smaller.
>He's shrinkin' there in front of me.
>Near to disappear ...
>The decider.
>And I had a dream ...

* * *

[Scene Change – DINNY's dream sequence]

[SFX: Music of Mise Éire by Seán Ó Ríada]
[The juxtaposition of the DINNY's Martin Luther King-esque style speech to fit pace of Mise Éire is the desired effect.
Fade to low. At end of scene. DINNY snaps back to reality]
[LX: Strong gold when FATHER is dazzled by glitter and gold]

DINNY:

> I had a dream…
> Yes sir-ee, I had a dream.
> And I'm standin' there,
> in the Parochial Hall.
> With the School's Championship trophy – glitterin' gold –
> held high in the air.
> Me dad's lookin' up at me.

FATHER:

> The main man!

DINNY:

> In sunglasses, all thumbs in the air
> and he's smilin' at me.

FATHER:

> Doubt ya Dinny boy!

DINNY:

> Why the sun glasses, Dad?

FATHER:

> 'Tis de glare, Dinny boy! 'Tis de glare!

DINNY:

> I had a dream,
> Ah, yes sir-ee! I had a dream.
> I could see it there…
> The School's Championship trophy, in my house on top of my
> telly.
>
> I had a dream! You better believe I had a dream …
>
> Me dad in sunglasses, all thumbs in the air,

dazzled by the glitter and the gold,
baskin' in the glare …

FATHER:
'Tis de glare! Dinny boy! 'Tis de glare!

DINNY:
I had a dream! Yes sir-ee I had a dream!
He's baskin' in the glitter and the glory.
And they're carrying me shoulder high,
through the streets of Cork.
Past the chicken chokers across Gurranabraher
And down to Linehan's sweet factory.

I had a dream!
Where everything is wonderful and happy in the world.

I had a dream yes sir-ee, I had a dream …
And my mam and my dad are holdin' hands.
They're lookin' up at me …
an' smilin' at one another …

FATHER: [proud]
My boy, Dinny boy. My boy …

[SFX: Fade down Mise Éire]
I had a dream…
Yes! I had a dream.

* * *

[Transition – back to reality of the Table Tennis at the Parochial Hall]

DINNY: *[back in reality]*
> ..and I can see yer man from St. Coleman's the far end a' the
> table.
> And I'm starin' him int've the eyes.
> And he's shrinkin' there.
> He's shrivellin' up,
> near to disappear.

FATHER: *[gently]*
> Gowan, Dinny boy!

DINNY:
> Yer man from St. Coleman's still shrinkin', shiverin', swayin'
> there …
>
> *[plays Table tennis]*
> Dish! Dish! Dish!

FATHER:
> 16-14!
> You can take him, Dinny boy!

DINNY:
> Definitely on a roll!
> Dish! Dish! Dish!

FATHER:
> 17-14, to the Mon.

DINNY:
> You're dead boy. Still my serve.
> Dish! Dish! Dish!

FATHER:
> 18-14! You have him, Dinny boy!

You have him!

DINNY:

Don't mess with the best!
Dish! Dish! Dish!

FATHER:

19-14! You can do it, Son!

FATHER & DINNY:

[to be sung, to the air of the Welsh hymn, 'Bread of Heaven']
Doubt ya, Dinny! Doubt ya, Dinny! Doubt ya, Dinny Keegan boy!
Doubt ya, Dinny! Doubt ya, Dinny! Doubt ya, Dinny Keegan boy!

DINNY:

This ones for you, Dad!

FATHER: *[pride/whisper]*
My boy …

DINNY:

I steady up,
Yer man from St. Coleman's, he's standing there.
Still shrinking there near to disappear.
I can see the fear in his eyes.

[gentle]
Shhhh! Shhhh!

Silence, Not a sound right across the Parochial Hall.
Nothing between me and victory except this paper ball.
Shhhh!
Total silence – and that's all.

Grip my bat,
ball rises to the sky like a paper moon.
Up past the haze.
Up past the haze of open-mouthed faces.
Like a dream – like a dream come true.

Then a face in the crowd …

FATHER: *[roars – upsets* DINNY'S *concentration]*
Pull on it man!

DINNY:
… and that's all.

Clung to the net.
No, Dad! No!

FATHER:
Get in close, will ya!

DINNY:
I steady up.
Shhhh …

My final serve.
Shhh …

FATHER: *[roar]*
Jesus Christ, Dinny boy!
In close and pull on the fuckin' thing!

DINNY: *[moves as if playing tennis]*
Dish! Dish! Dish!
16-19
No dad!

FATHER:

> Yer lettin' it slip away!

DINNY:

> 17-19.

FATHER:

> For fuck's sake, Dinny boy!
> This is the North Mon yer playin' for!

DINNY:

> No, Dad!

FATHER:

> In close! In fuckin' close!

DINNY:

> No, Dad! No!

FATHER:

> An' pull on the gruntin' thing!

DINNY:

> Don't do this to me, Dad!
> 18-19

FATHER:

> For grunt's sake, Dinny boy! For grunt's sake!

DINNY:

> 19-All.

FATHER:

> Grunt somethin' will ya! Grunt on the gruntin' ball will ya!

DINNY:

 20-19.

FATHER:

 Jesus Christ! What are ya at out there, man!
 Grunt on the gruntin' ball! Will ya!
 Grunt on the gruntin' grunt, Dinny! Grunt man!
 Grunt!

DINNY:

 21-19.

 [totally defeated]
 Game, set and match to St. Coleman's Fermoy…

FATHER: *[total despair]*
 God al-gruntin'-mighty!

[Transition – DINNY to REFEREE]
[REFEREE looks up at his FATHER, feeling totally rejected]

REFEREE:

 My dad went back to gruntin' – gruntin' around the house …

FATHER:

 Grunt!

REFEREE:

 Gruntin' around the house right up to the day he died.

FATHER:

 Grunt! Grunt! Grunt!

REFEREE:

 … and he did,

another three years gruntin'.
Die that is…

And they layin' him to rest,
his coffin carried down, beneath an arch of crossed hurleys.
Glen Rovers jersey draped across his chest.

Great sports man, they said.
He lived for the hurlin'.
He lived for the hurlin'.

He's not two days in the grave and my mam gives me a
football.
My first big ball.
Jeezus.
And I played soccer.

FATHER:
[Spirit of FATHER staring out at the audience – barking out words]
 A namby-pamby's game!

REFEREE:
 Fit. Fast.
 It was like, I could stop the ball – but I couldn't deliver.
 I could dive – but I couldn't save.
 I could jump – but I couldn't header.

FATHER:
 Textbook expert!

REFEREE:
 At sixteen,
 too long in the teeth to teach these feet what to do.
 Runnin' up and down, up and down, up and down.

FATHER:

>Without a smell of the ball!
>He'll serve his time, Missus!

REFEREE:

>I served my time, Dad!
>Cup Final day – big as it gets.
>And I'll be out there.
>Keepin' up with play!

FATHER:

>Piggy in the miggle!

REFEREE:

>Keepin up with play with lads half my age!

[REFEREE checking his equipment]
[REFEREE is trying to get FATHER's taunts out of his mind]

>Whistle? Check!
>Red card? Check!
>Yellow card? Check!
>I've served my time, Dad!

FATHER:

>He'll serve his time Missus!

REFEREE:

>Notebook? Check!
>Pen? Check!
>Body: battered, bruised and bloody …

FATHER:

>Christy Ring never wore a helmet!

REFEREE:

Watch? Check!

FATHER:

Boil me head in Parazone!

REFEREE:

I've served my time.

FATHER:

Only the girls and Chineee.

REFEREE:

And I played hurlin'.
I could have been the next Christy Ring!

FATHER:

Could have been?
Could have been ...

REFEREE: *[losing control/upset]*

I am the man!
Out there! Out there!
The fittest man on the field. Coverin' every blade of grass.
Eyes in the back a' me head!
Watchin'. Listenin'.
Runnin' up and down, up and down, up and down ...
Out there I'm the man.
They mess with me. They're off the field!

[REFEREE losing control]

* * *

[Scene Change – back to the FAI CUP Final – second half]
[SFX: Fade up crowd]

[Transition – FATHER to COMMENTATOR]

COMMENTATOR:

. . . and the teams expected back on the pitch any second now for the second half of this the FAI Cup Final.

REFEREE: *[upset]*

I've served my time, Dad!
Are ya listenin' to me, Dad!
I've served me time.

They listen to me.

They listen to the man.
Out there today, I am the man!
The judge and jury!

[SFX: fade up the crowd – crowd react to logic of game as described by COMMENTATOR – throughout the COMMENTATOR's commentary, REFEREE's spiralling manic intensity becomes obvious by his series, of stylised movements, hand actions, intense staring, whistle blowing etc.]

COMMENTATOR:

Oooh! What a magnificent interception by Murray the big centre–back for City.
The pace of this second half has certainly picked up.
Must have been some strong words in the dressing room.
Murray – plays it to O'Callaghan.
Kearney runnin' in – oough!

[REFEREE – blows whistle – shows yellow card]

REFEREE: *[slightly manic]*

Player! Player!
I'm on to you!
You're like a horse around the box.

You pull another stunt like that ...
You're off the field!

COMMENTATOR:

Referee Dino Keegan stamping his authority on this game.
And it' a high ball into the Shelburne half.
Doyle volleys it.
Oough! It's deflected by the keeper out over the end-line.

REFEREE: *[stylised REFEREE movement and appropriate hand signal]*
[Whistle]
Corner ball!
[Whistle]

COMMENTATOR:

Kearney sends a long ball swinging in across the box ...
Keeper comin' off his line...
Flapping for the ball...
Behan rising up for it, connects with the head ...
Oough! Just inches wide of the upright.

[Whistle]
[REFEREE indicates goal kick]

COMMENTATOR:

And once again O'Callaghan's pushing forward,
takes his man on...
And that was a dangerous late tackle on O'Callaghan...

REFEREE: *[stylised hand movement]*
Play on! Play on!

COMMENTATOR:

Advantage played! Excellent decision by Dino Keegan.
O'Callaghan still on his feet. Battling his way through the

defence …

[Referee whistle and hand movement]

Kearney – a bit unlucky there,
appears to have handled the ball.
Quickly taken by Hawkins …

COMMENTATOR:
Shelburne on the break.
A beautiful ball played through the middle to Cahill.
Cahill to Crowe.
He turns! He shoots!
And - what a sensational save, sending Devine to full stretch
to keep the ball out of the net.
A scramble in the box and a frantic clearance by Billy Woods
…

[Referee whistle and hand movement]

REFEREE:
Throw ball!

COMMENTATOR:
And as we're counting down the dying seconds in this FAI
Cup Final.
And following what was a scrappy first half.
This game has come alive!
Both teams pushing forward.
It's attacking all the time.

COMMENTATOR:
And it's a long ball down the wing – John O' Flynn running in.

[Referee whistle and hand movement]

COMMENTATOR:

>And it's a free kick just on the edge of the box.
>a last chance for City.
>After ninety minutes of deadlock,
>City putting every man forward for this one.
>Keeper frantically reorganising his wall.
>This must be the last kick of the game.
>Dino Keegan once again checking his watch…

[REFEREE whistle and hand movement]

COMMENTATOR:

>Behan stepping forward to take it.
>He's standing over the ball now.
>The tension building around the stadium,
>Keeper once again checking his wall …
>
>He sends it high.
>Ball swinging out…

[LX: sharp light on REFEREE]

REFEREE:

>I can see the ball…
>I can see the ball, and that's all!
>And behind, a haze of faces.
>Time's up in the FAI Cup.
>I can see the ball and it's dipping down,
>Shhhh! Shhhh!
>I'm the Hand King …
>
>I can see the ball, and that's all …
>And behind the haze of faces …
>Time's up in the FAI Cup …

And it's dropping down.
No more judge. No more jury!

And it's droppin' down to me?

No more Referee!

[Slow motion – strobe light : REFEREE volleys the ball into the back of the net]
[SFX – thud of ball being kicked][SFX – crowd roar]

COMMENTATOR: *[highly excited – over SFX crowd roaring]*
    What a Gooooal! Goal! Goal!
    Referee Dino Keegan has just scored what must be the goal of the season!

[REFEREE stands there, hands raised to the crowd in victory – basking in the glory]
[SFX – crowd]

[COMMENTATOR continues to talk in a very excited fashion, his commentary gradually fades as the sound of the crowd fades]

COMMENTATOR: *[garbled commentary drowned out by sound of crowd]*
    And after ninety minutes of such drab and lifeless football, who could ever have anticipated it would end this way.
    What a sensational goal by referee Dino Keegan.
    A man who is retiring from the game. Hanging up his whistle so to speak, a man who has devoted much of his life to the game of soccer … [fade]

[SFX: fade the sound of COMMENTATOR – fade the sound of the crowd]
[FX: slowly fade up evocative slow piano or childlike music box]

[REFEREE *stands there alone centre stage in a spotlight*]

REFEREE: [*pathetic almost child-like/tearful*]
     Did ya see that, Dad! Did ya see me, Dad!
     Hand eye and ball coordination.

     I am the man.
     The main man.

     Dad?
     Did ya see me Daddy?

     Daddy …

[*SFX: fade music*]
[*LX: fade to black*]

THE END

After Luke

BY

Cónal Creedon

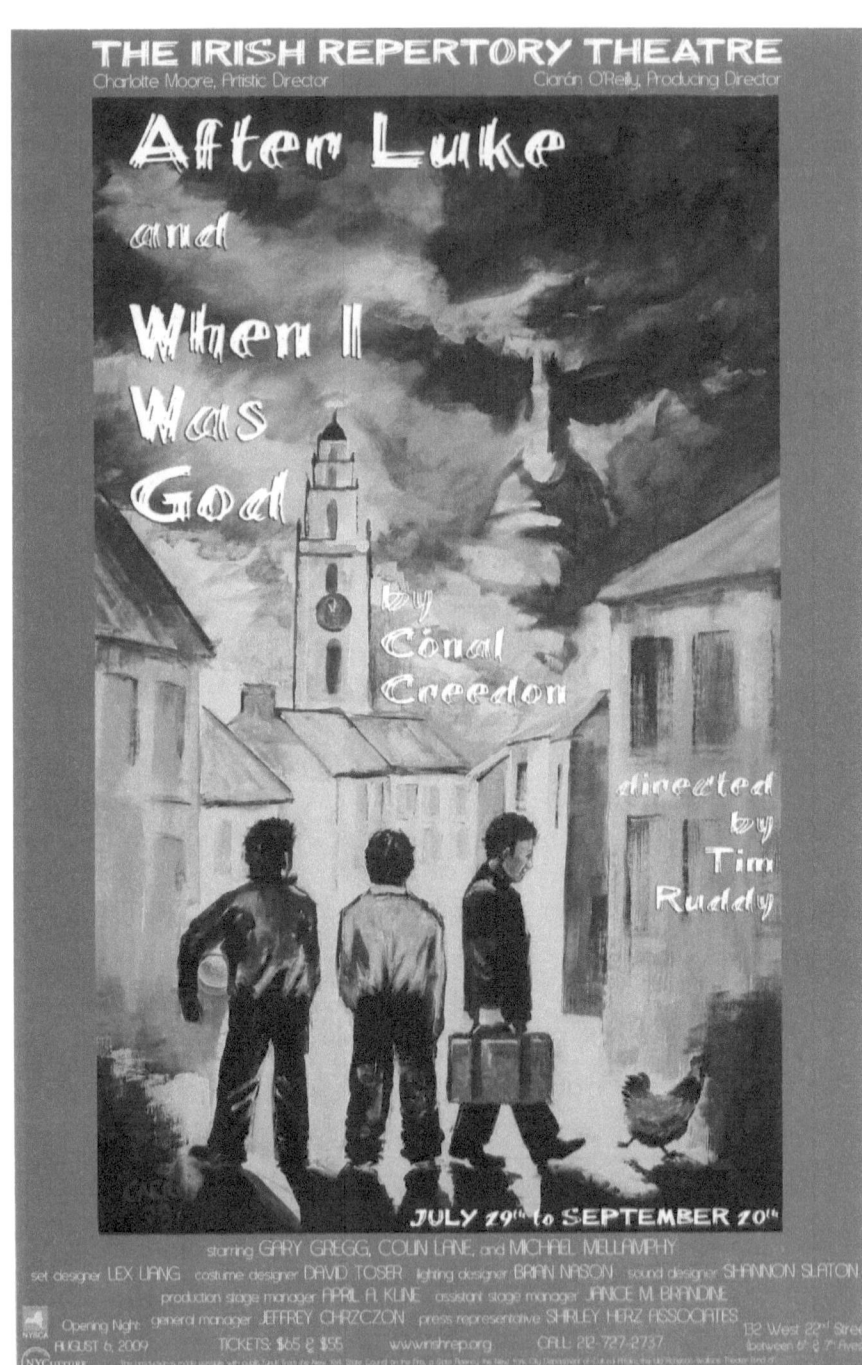

AFTER LUKE

AFTER LUKE is inspired by St. Luke's parable, The Prodigal Son.
Set during the wild property book during the Celtic Tiger Economy.
The play explores father/son relationships and is set against the
economic boom in Ireland. After Luke examines how a perceived
escalation of property value may be the catalyst for a severe reaction
between two brothers – SON and MANEEN – particularly when the
property in question happens to be the family home.

Cast: Three male actors.
One actor aged mid 50s to 60s will play DADDA.
A second actor aged 40s will play SON.
A third actor aged 30's will play two parts : MANEEN and MRS FOLEY.

MANEEN is the younger brother. He is worldly and flash. He wants
to get out of the home place – attracted by bright lights / big city. He
wants the quick buck.
SON's view of life is a lot simpler. He doesn't like change – He likes
things done the way they've always been done. He is content to work
in their father's car parts business –happiest when he's out in the yard
stripping down cars.

Minimal set. No props. Suggest two plinths of different levels.
There are many locations required in the play, [chicken shed, yard,
kitchen, downtown, in car, Foley's shop etc.]. These locations are
not identified by set – but should be clearly defined and marked as
locations within the play

[Notes: Because this play is set in a sort of a time warp of timelessness – both old time and modern values should be enhanced. Suggest that MANEEN is costumed in a suit typical of the Dagenham Yanks 50s style. Maybe DADDA wears a similar suit – but more threadbare and shiny around the knees & elbows. Son to wear a mechanic's grubby oily overalls – beneath the overalls – a very clean white shirt and pressed trousers – for the transformation scene when he decided to ask PEGGY FOLEY out on a date.

After Luke – is structured almost like a court case – where all three characters who have difficulty in expressing their feelings to each other – speak directly to the audience as if pleading their case]

MANEEN: *[directly to audience]*
>   Sell the fuckin' place!
>   Listen to me now, Dad.
>   Ten years ago you couldn't give this place away.
>   But these days?
>   These days it's worth a fortune …
>   I mean Jesus, you could …

SON: *[directly to audience]*
[In chicken shed]
>   Chalk and cheese.
>   Don't get me wrong now, I love me brother.
>   But every time he comes home – he drives me …
>   Still not in the better of his last visit.
>   Turned the whole place upside down and inside out
>   – so he did.

DADDA: *[In Kitchen]*
[Walks down stage – whistles as if calling dog]
>   *[shout]* Son! Here Son!
>   Son!
>   *[whisper]* For Christ's sake …
>   *[shout]* Son!
>   *[whistles again]*

SON: *[directly to audience - not responding to DADDA]*
[In chicken shed]
>   And Dadda? A bigger eejit to be listenin' to him.
>   Even the last time he was home,
>   I knew they were up to somethin'.
>   Sittin' here watchin' the two of 'em,
>   inside the kitchen there – hugger-muggerin'

MANEEN: [directly to audience]
>For God sake, Dad …
>You could build half a dozen houses out in that yard there.
>I mean, Jesus! 'Tis worth more as a site than it is a house!
>Knock it and flog it!
>Yer sittin' on a gold mine!
>
>Look there's a fella I know –
>an estate agent.
>Just let him come up.
>He'll tell ya what the place is worth.
>But Jesus, ya gotta strike while the iron's hot, Dad!

* * *

SON: [directly to audience]
>Even when we were young fellas – out here in the yard –
>cowboys and Indians …

* * *

[Transition to vignette of past – when they were kids – SON and MANEEN are obviously in a stand-off situation]

DADDA: [enters scene – furious – a fury that is mirrored at end of play]
>Jesus Christ! Will ye just cut it out, will ye!
>Yer' mother's spinnin' like a top in her grave with ye!
>Just cut it out!

MANEEN: [childish – defensive]
>But he started it, Dadda!

[SON looking innocent and confused]

DADDA:
> I don't care who started what! Just cut it out!
>
> *[speaking directly to SON]*
> Now, what are ya after doin' to him?

SON:
> Me, Dadda? Nothin'!

DADDA:
> You must be after doin' something!

SON:
> It's him! He won't die, Dadda …

DADDA:
> How do ya mean he won't die?

SON:
> I'm after shootin' him loads a times and he just won't die!

[DADDA is confused - looks to MANEEN]

MANEEN:
> Cochise, Dadda!

DADDA:
> Hah?

MANEEN:
> Cochise!

DADDA:

Cochise what?

MANEEN:

Cochise - the war chief!
You know the Sioux!

DADDA:

And who are you?

MANEEN:

General Custer …

SON:

… an he's supposed to die, Dadda!
It's Custer's last stand and he's supposed to …

MANEEN:

Sur' Cochise wasn't even at Custer's last stand!
Everybody knows 'twas – Sittin' Bull!

SON:

It don't matter – you're suppose to die!

DADDA:

Christ almighty! Will ye stop!
I spend me whole life tryin' to keep the two a'ye apart.
Look, you're older than him, you'd think you'd have more
sense.
Now for a quiet life, couldn't ya let him live this once, just this
once …

SON:

But it happens every time – he just keeps changin' the rules.

MANEEN:

Cochise speaks with forked tongue, Dadda.

SON:

And what about the chicken shed …

DADDA:

Chicken shed?

SON:

He's after drivin' me outa the chicken shed, Dadda.
I'm the one who looks after the chickens …

[DADDA *looks to* MANEEN *for an explanation*]

MANEEN:

He's an Indian, Dadda!
Indians always get driven offa' their land!
Every one knows that …

SON:

Not fair, Dadda – it's wrong!

DADDA:

Look two wrongs don't make a right!
You're older than him you should have more sense.

* * *

SON: [*directly to audience*]
Always lived in me small brother's shadow …

DADDA: [*whistle as if calling a dog*]
Son! Here, Son!

Son! For Christ's sake, Son –

SON: [directly to audience]
>Even on me Confirmation Day.
>Two months after his First Holy Communion.
>He still peacocking around the place.
>Still wearin' the bánín suit – rosette, sash the lot!
>Peacocking around the place with the hand out.
>
>And everybody saying how cute he looked in his new suit.
>Like a little Maneen – in the long pants – with the hand out.
>Makin' a fortune on the back of my Confirmation.
>And he still with the Holy Communion money in his back
>pocket …

* * *

[Transition to vignette of past – when they were kids – once again SON
and MANEEN are obviously in a stand-off situation]

DADDA:
>Ah, Jesus what's wrong with ye now!

MANEEN:
>He got more money than me, Dadda!

SON: [pleading]
>It's my Confirmation money.

DADDA:
>How much did ya get?

SON:
>Five pounds fifty-two new pence.

DADDA:

And you?

MANEEN:

Three pounds seventy-five, Dadda.

SON:

But he still have his Holy Communion money!
[MANEEN looks innocent as SON pleads]
He do, Dadda! He do!

DADDA:

Look the best thing now – is for you to give yer small brother
a pound.
Then ye'll have four pound fifty a man.

SON:

But he still have his Holy Communion money...

DADDA:

That's my final word on it!

SON:

It's not fair, Dadda ...

DADDA:

Well life's not fair, Son.
I spend me whole life standing between the two of ye.
Look you're older – you should have more sense –
now - for a quiet life just give him the pound!
Just give him the pound, will ya!

***

SON: [directly to audience]
I've always lived in me small brother's shadow – and that don't bother me.

***

MANEEN: [directly to audience]
Cork? Cork'd do yer fuckin' head in.
Like 'twas clamped in a vice.
Just closin' in on me –
twistin' and twistin'.

Don't get me wrong now – I love my brother,
but Jesus he drives me!
Like he's livin' in the past.
Still shoppin' in Foley's shop.
Still droppin' me dad to the bingo.
Still doin' things the way they've always been done.
Livin' in a time warp …
I had to get the hell outa there.

And Dadda? [hissed] Jeezus!
Even when we were young fellas …

***

[Transition to vignette from the past – when they were kids]
[DADDA and SON are examining a screw - MANEEN attempts to be part of the conversation.]

DADDA:

Son, come here, la? Do ya see that there?
That's a special cross-headed, spring release grip screw …

SON:

A spring release grip screw, Dadda?

DADDA:

That's right…

MANEEN:

Can I see it, Dadda?

DADDA:

Ah, Jesus Maneen, stay back you'll only get hurt!

[To SON]
See Son, the more ya screw it this way.
That little spring releases the grip on the far side,
for the bushing on the manifold …

MANEEN:

Show us, Dad?

DADDA:

Look Maneen – You're only getting' in the way out here.

MANEEN: *[directly to audience - remembering DADDA's words]*
Go up to the house there like a good boy!

And that don't bother me …
That's what happens when yer the runt of a family.

It's Christmas. I'm sittin' under the tree. Delighted with meself.
A spanking new cowboy suit, sheriff's badge, hat, waistcoat,

six-guns, spurs –
the works.
Then I see Son – his eyes poppin' outa' his head.
Face lit up by – by the gleaming steel.
Spanners and screwdrivers and pliers – wrenches and sockets,
all neatly lined up in their own little pockets.
And after the turkey
me Dad stands up …

DADDA:

Son! Come on out to the yard.
We'll christen that toolbox.
I'll show ya how to strip down a gearbox …

Maneen:
Listenin' to the two a' them outside in the yard
havin' a good aul' laugh.
And I'm sittin' in me cowboy suit, all on me own,
For the rest of Christmas Day…

* * *

SON: [directly to audience]
And what about the time me Dad got a Ford's box.
Puts it on a site down Myrtleville, for the summer holidays …
And I'm building a sand castle,
all towers, and moats, and turrets.
Like a Disneyland version of Blarney and Blackrock Castle.
The most amazing castle you ever seen.

And who comes along? Who comes along? Maneen!
Like Myrtleville beach wasn't big enough for him.
He had to build his castle – slap bang right next to mine.
Like a fuckin' semi-d.

...nothing would do him but to break through my wall.
And I'm sayin' –
No, Maneen! No! 'Tis a huge beach!
There's plenty of sand over there!
No, Maneen! No!

DADDA:

What are ya at now, Son?!

[MANEEN looks innocent]
Well Jesus, ya must be doing something – 'cause he's cryin'!

SON:

No, Maneen! No!

DADDA:

Isn't the beach big enough! Couldn't you go way over there
somewhere –
and don't be annoyin' him…

SON:

But I built that castle there, Dadda …

DADDA:

I don't give a fiddler's fart who built what where!
– there's plenty a' sand for everyone.
Now go on, get over there – and build yer bloody sandcastle!
Jesus! You're the oldest– ya should have more sense!

SON: *[directly to audience]*

And then he gets sunburned – I get blamed.
And he gets stung by the jellyfish – I get blamed.
And when he nearly drowns …
Maneen gets dragged out by the current.
Next stop the Gulf of Mexico …

Without even thinkin' how much easier my life would be if he
was to vanish forever to the depths of the big blue sea –
I jumps in after him – with no concern for my own health or
safety!
Drags him out by the hair –
And he splutterin', gaspin' for air.

DADDA:

Will ya stop pullin' yer bother's hair!

SON:

But he nearly got drowned, Dadda!

DADDA:

Jesus Christ! I'll drown you if yer not careful!

SON: [directly to audience]

Saved his life, and I get blamed …
And ya know?
That don't bother me …

* * *

[Transition to present]

DADDA: [whistle as if calling a dog]

Son!
Here, Son! For Christ's sake, Son!
We'll be late for the bingo!
Son!
Do I have to walk down on me own or what!

SON: [directly to audience]

Don't get me wrong - I love my brother,

But Jesus, when Maneen fucked off to London there ten years
ago, tellin' ya –
'twas like a weight offa' my shoulders.
Now I wasn't too happy with Dadda selling the Ford's box.
But if it meant that Maneen was outa my hair …

MANEEN: [directly to audience]
Drawn to London, like a, like a moth to a lamp –
Bright lights, big city, wild nights.
Dreamin' a' them Soho sluts – All powder, an' rouge, an' waxy
lips?

And fair dues to Dadda, now …
He sold the Ford's box – see me on me way, like.

So when I first hit London town – I hit the place runnin'.
Money in the pocket – wasn't hurtin'.
D'ya know what I mean. Pocket full a cash.
Head full a dreams. What more do ya need?

But London? London ates money.
Went through me like, like piss-water in a drunk.
Met a fella down Brixton, fella from home.
Tells me to go up to Dagenham.
Says his brother's hirin'.
Tell him where yer from who sent ya and everything be –
Sound boy! Sound! Sorted!

Says,
Dagenham's like, it's like little Cork.
Beamish Stout, Evergreen sausages and Barry's tea …
Go down! Half the town's down there.
Followin' week!
Half eight – at the gate! Be there!

Sound boy! Sound! Sorted! Alright?!
Cushy number!
Clock in – Clock out – wage packet of a Friday!

* * *

DADDA: *[to SON]*
God Almighty, I'm hoarse from callin' ya!

SON:
Just finishin' up a few things around the yard.
A fella callin' back for the wing mirror offa' that 280E …
[DADDA looks confused]
The Merc!
[DADDA shows recognition]
And a one in this mornin' lookin' for the back door offa the
Honda Civic.

DADDA:
Out there earlier – didn't see ya nowhere …

SON:
Down the chicken shed.

DADDA:
Never understand the fascination you has for them chickens.

SON:
Ah, sur' they're a bit a company…

DADDA:
The chickens? Company?
[whisper] Fuck's sake?

SON:

    Intelligent beast the chicken.
    I mean you take Reddy there …

DADDA:

    Who?

SON:

    Reddy!
    You know, the one I got there lately …

DADDA:

    … all chickens look the same to me, Son.

SON:

    Not at all!
    Ah ya gotta be able to get inside the brain of a chicken,
    Dadda …

DADDA:

    Inside – the brain – of a chicken?

SON:

    Chalk it down, Dadda!
    Reddy? She's a bright spark.
    Might be as daft as a duck …
    But she'd read yer mind – that one.

    And cars?
    What that chicken don't know about cars isn't worth knowin'.
    She just sits there long-side me all day – every day,
    watchin' everythin' I do.
    Every turn of a bolt and twist of a screw.

Sure even earlier today – and I taking out a fuel pump –
the screw slipped down between the carburettor and the
sump.
Like a flash, boy! Reddy was in under the car – got the screw
and brought it back out to me.
Tellin' ya –

If she'd fingers instead a feathers
she'd make a handy mechanic …

DADDA:

The chicken?

SON:

Chalk it down, Dadda!

DADDA: [unamused]

Come on – fer fuck's sake – drive us down to the bingo – will
ya?!

* * *

MANEEN: [directly to audience]

Clock in – Clock out! Wage packet of a Friday!
Down Dagenham.
Living in a kip.
Pushin' levers for a livin'.
Lookin' for me hole.
Pissin' me wages up against a wall.
Them Soho sluts wouldn't touch me with a 10-foot barge pole.

And I'm thinkin' of home.
And what really does my head in.
I'm Dadda's son. Not him!

And I'm down here in Dagenham town –
Like I'm squeezed out.
Squeezed out by the golden boy. The chosen one …

And factory work? Factory work is donkey work –
Payday Friday.
Drunk 'til Sunday.
Broke by Monday.
Climbin' the walls by Thursday …
Clock in! Clock out!
Wage packet of a Friday!

And I'm thinkin' of Dadda …
I'm thinkin' of me half-brother the half-wit.
Over there in Cork. Sittin' on a goldmine

of rusting cars and chicken shit.
And I'm thinkin' of home …

* * *

*[SON and DADDA sitting side by side as if in a car. They are under lit –
as if dash-board lights - The car is freewheeling and DADDA is furious.]*

DADDA: *[angry]*
For Christ's sake, Son!
Slap her int've gear will ya!
Son!
Slap her int've gear! Will ya!

SON:
Sur' I always freewheel down to the bingo, Dadda!

DADDA:

> Slap her int've gear! Will ya!
> You'll make shit a' the gear-box!

SON:

> Speed bump!

[SON and DADDA bounce off their seats – due to car hitting speed bump]

DADDA:

> Jesus!
> You'll shatter the suspension and make shit of the gear-box!
> Slap her int've gear will ya!
> What the hell is wrong with ya! Hah!
> Couldn't ya drive the car like a normal person.

SON:

> Sur', there last week I freewheeled all the way from our house
> – down Ol' Youghal Road – the length of Ballyhooley Road
> across the back of Mayfield all the way down to the Glen Hall
> without even turnin' the key!
> I mean Jesus, that was some feat all the same, hah?!

DADDA:

> Be some fuckin' feat if ya made shit of the gear-box.

DADDA: *[directly to audience]*
[DADDA is sitting in passenger seat of car. This is an internal monologue. Every now and then he casts a cynical eye at SON who is content to be freewheeling down to bingo.]

> [whisper] Jesus Christ?
> How in the name of Christ did I rear a half-wit?
> A good lad. Don't drink. Don't smoke.
> Never had as much as an ounce a trouble outa' him –
> Strip a car down to the chassis in a half a day, so he would.
> Happiest out tinkering with cars? And how bad …

SON:

>Speed bump!

[DADDA *and* SON *bounce out of their seat – due to car hitting speed bump*]
DADDA: [*direct to audience - internal monologue*]

>How bad indeed?
>Brain of a mechanic – the hands of a surgeon.
>The other fella? Maneen?
>They're like chalk and cheese. Chalk and cheese.
>Maneen's as bright as a button. Up there he have it.

[DADDA *is snapped back to present as he sees a cyclist in front of car*]
[*to* SON]

>Mind the cyclist, Son!
>The fella on the bike!
>[urgent] Mind the fella on the bike, will ya!

[DADDA *and* SON *move as if the car had to swerve to miss the cyclist – they look behind them as they speed pass the cyclist*]
DADDA:

>Jeezus!

SON:

>Speed bump!

[SON *and* DADDA *hop off seats and swerve*]
DADDA:

>Christ's sake, Son!
>Jesus!

[*directly to audience – internal monologue*]

>I love when Maneen comes home for the holidays.
>Miss him around the place, so ya would.
>A bit of a spark about Maneen.

Then again...
Chalk and cheese? Chalk it down!

[DADDA *does not engage with* SON'*s chatter in the background*]
SON: [*to* DADDA – *but* DADDA *is preoccupied with his own internal thoughts*]
>Tellin' ya Dadda –
>I saw the maddest thing yesterday and I comin' across Christy Ring Bridge,
>Yer not gonna believe this.
>I saw The first black Echo boy!
>I mean what d'ya make a that Dadda?
>[DADDA does not answer]
>Dadda?!

DADDA: [*being snapped out of his internal thoughts*]
>Eh, sorry, Son! Sorry!
>What's that you were sayin', Son?

SON:
>The first black Echo boy, Dadda!

DADDA: [*startled - looks around him*]
>What? Where?

SON:
>No, no yesterday –

DADDA: [*looks confused*]

SON:
>Standin' in the middle a' Christy Ring Bridge!

DADDA:
>A black fella?

SON:

Sellin' the Evenin' Echo – if ya don't mind …

DADDA:

A black fella sellin' the Echo …

SON:

Tellin' ya, we're in Europe now, Dadda.

DADDA:

True for ya Son. True for ya. …

[identifying a parking space]
Look! There, look! Son! There!

SON:

Here is it, Dadda?

DADDA: *[DADDA directing SON to a parking space]*
Ya can park the car in there, la.

SON:

There?

DADDA:

Ah Christ, 'tis gone – there la! There!

SON:

Where?

DADDA:

Jesus there!
There's another space there! That's gone too! There la!

SON:

Here?

DADDA:

There la!

SON:

Here is it?

DADDA: [becoming agitated frustrated/angry]

Ah, for Christ's sake put a bush in the gap, will ya!
And park the shaggin' car! Will ya!
Jezzus! Look! Just pull up the car – and let me out!
Let me out! Will ya!

SON:

How's that, Dadda?

DADDA: [aggravated calm]

… that's fine, Son! Just fine.
You'll be here when I come out won't ya, Son?

SON:

I'll be here for ya, Dadda.

DADDA: [DADDA stands up as if getting out of car]
Good lad, Son. Good lad …

* * *

SON: [directly to audience – sitting in car alone]
Tuesday night – is the best day a the week.
An' this time a' the evenin'? Is the best part a' the day.
See Tuesday night – is bingo night in our house.

Lashes back the tea – hops into the car.
Freewheels down to the Glen Hall. Pulls up outside the bingo.

Dadda melts with the crowd and vanishes into the hall.
I cut across t've Foley's to pick up the weeks messages.
And there's something about Foley's shop?
Maybe 'tis the Vapona,
or the way they have the coal bags stacked outside the counter.
Maybe 'tis that they do thing the way they've always been
done.
Tinkle – tinkle – tinkle! The shop doorbell!

[Transition – Maneen *to* Mrs Foley*]*

Mrs Foley:

    Well how are you, Sonny, and it must be Tuesday night if 'tis
    yerself …

Son: *[directly to audience]*

    That's what Mrs Foley always says.

Mrs Foley:

    I could set me clock by ya.
    [shrill/shout] Martina! Martina!

Son: *[directly to audience]*

    Like clockwork. Mrs Foley crows it out.

Mrs Foley:

    [shrill/shout] Martina! Martina!

[She reads Son's *shopping list sounds like a mantra]*

    2 lbs. of butter –
    2 lbs. of sugar –
    2 lbs. a' tea –

2 lbs. a' blackberry jam.
Four loaves a' bread.
A package a' Kimberly biscuits,
and a half pound of Evergreen sausages for the breakfast on
Sunday.

SON:

That's right Mrs Foley.

MRS FOLEY:

[shrill] Martina! Martina!

SON:

An' out steps Martina – Mrs Foley's daughter.
Out from the kitchen.
An' she taking off her apron – an' adjusting her hair.
And while Mrs Foley is making up me messages –
Meself and Martina talk.

[MARTINA comes onto SON in a playful way – this is something she does every week. And because of SON's innocence – we're not fully sure if she has genuine intentions towards SON or is she just playing with him. But there is a sense that SON and MARTINA are the only two of their specific type in the parish – both past the first flush of youth. Both staying at home working with elderly parents – so MARTINA may be resigned to the idea that Son might be the 'best' she can get.]

She asks me how're my chickens –
So, I tell her the latest episode from the escapades of Reddy,
– Super hen!
She says she'd love to come up and see them sometime …
I tell her, I'd be delighted if she'd come up and see them … –
Sometime.

We talk about everythin'. Everythin' and nothin'.

I gives Martina half a dozen eggs for her father's breakfast.
She says my eggs are the sweetest eggs in the city.

Then she points to a poster on the side of the fridge.
And says that Daniel O' Donnell is givin' a concert in town on
Thursday week.
And she asks me do I have any plans for Thursday week.

Thursday week? No Martina.
No plans for Thursday week.
But sur' Thursday week's almost, well it's almost two weeks
away.

Then Mrs Foley arrives over …

MRS FOLEY:

You'll have to remind me, Sonny
Is it Barry's or Lyons's –
the tea like?

SON:

Oh, Barry's best Mrs Foley – me dad won't drink nothin' else.
An' fair dues to Martina now, she always have the few
newspapers left over from the week rolled up and stuffed
down the side a me messages.

I lift up the box off the counter. Martina opens the shop door
…

Tinkle – tinkle – tinkle. And close it behind me …

Sit int've the car.
Switch on the radio.

[SON switches on the radio – SFX: C&W Irish music]

Stretch out the paper across the passenger seat.
And wait for Dadda to come outa the bingo.

As I say now…
Tuesday night is the best day a the week.
And this time a' the evening is the best part a' the day …

* * *

[Transition – MRS FOLEY to MANEEN]

MANEEN: *[directly to audience]*
Tuesday night – talking shite,
with two fellas – three times my age.
Hidin' in a haze of cigarette smoke …
Same faces – same places.
Lined up along the bar – like a man.

And these four burst through the door like they own the place.

One glance in the mirror – I had 'em pegged.
Four fuckin' computer geniuses –
or insurance – or stockbrokers,
or the fuckin' BBC – or some place like that.
And as soon as they opened their mouth I could tell,
two, or maybe three of them were from home …
By the cut a' their clothes – you'd know they were doin' well.

Like a human tornado – they were.
They were winding each other up and putting each other down.
Drinkin' tequila slammers and vodka and red bull.
Turning shit loads a' money and making too much noise.

Not that I was listening – but I could hear 'em –
Making too much noise about nothin'.

[Imitates posh boy accent] Property, investment, skiing
holidays –
One of 'em was talking about trekking through
the mountains in South America for three months.

Three fuckin' months! Paid a fortune for it he did –
eatin' out of tins, no toilets, no toilet paper, no hot water –
nothin' – cost him a fuckin' fortune…

[posh Cork accent]:'Twas all about endurance –

And I thinkin' to myself he should try living in my kip
for a few weeks – he'd know all about fuckin' endurance.

And women?
By all accounts, they had more women than you could shake a
stick at!
Batin' 'em off them they were.
And like that! [click fingers]
As quick as they came they were gone.

A few eyes around the bar turned to heaven.
Someone muttered fuckin' eejits!
And it was back to the same aul ding–dong.
But it crossed my mind – This was not the plan!
Maybe they were – fuckin' ejits!
But the life that they were living,
was exactly what brought me to London in the first place.
To be like them – livin' the life – turnin' the money.
Big city, wild nights, bright lights.

* * *

[DADDA sits into car]
DADDA: *[angry/abrupt]*
    Jesus Christ,
    how many times do I have to tell ya about the car radio –
    runnin' down the battery.
    Turn that fuckin' thing off – will ya!

[SON turns off the radio]
SON: *[look of despair]*

DADDA: *[gruff]*
    You picked up the messages!

SON:
    I did, Dadda.
    Talkin' to Martina too, so I was …

DADDA:
    Gowan, drive the car will ya!

SON:
    So eh, how did the bingo go?

DADDA: *[demoralised]*
    Key a' the door?

SON:
    What's tha', Dadda?

DADDA: *[building to frenzy]*
    Key a' the fuckin' door – twenty-one!
    Six full calls I was waitin' – two fat ladies – eighty-eight!
    Two little ducks – twenty-two!

Sweat! Jesus Christ, son, the sweat was pourin' outa me!
Kelly's eye – number-one!
Forty-five! – halfway home. Still waitin',
Waitin' on the key a the door for the full-house.
Legs eleven! An' I'm sittin' there an' I'm sweatin'.
Left an' right a me there's heads down
an' they're scratchin' their books.
An' I may as well be only scratchin' me hole!
Unlucky for some - thirteen!
'twas fuckin' unlucky for me, boy!
Next thing ya know? Next thing ya know!
Never been kissed before. Sweet-sixteen.
[roar] Check!

[Defeated] Sweet fuck all …
Foley?! 'Twas fuckin' Foley himself that took the shaggin'
jackpot!
Money always goes to them that has it! Hah!
An' I wouldn't mind but didn't I step back an' let him walk in
to the hall first, before me.
Jesus wept!
If I had only went ahead like I was – 'tis I'd have got the book
he got,
and I'd have the jackpot now! Jesus Christ all fuckin' mighty.

'Twas you!
You an' all your fartin' around outside –
tryin' to park the shaggin' car that delayed me – not to mind
you up talkin' to them shaggin' chickens of yours.
[Son appears emotionally battered]

Gowan, drive the fuckin' car will ya …

* * *

MANEEN: *[On the phone from London - to DADDA on the phone]*
  - Dadda?
  - Can ya talk?
  - Did yer man call up to look at the place?
  - The estate agent!
  - How much did he say it was worth?
  - How much! How much!
  - See what'd I tell ya! I told ya didn't I!
  - Wha'? Course ya should sell the place!
  - Why?
  - Son?
  - Fuck him, Dad! Fuck him!
  - Look, I'm comin' home!
  - I'm comin' home, alright!

* * *

DADDA: *[DADDA to SON - DADDA is obviously feeling awkward]*
  Oh, by the way, Son.
  I eh, meant to tell ya…
  Maneen phoned the other night …

SON: *[cautious]*
  Maneen?
  Is he alright?

DADDA:
  Oh, he's fine.
  Fine, fine, fine, fine, fine, fine, fine, fine ….
  Yeah, he's fine.

SON:

No news or nothin'?

DADDA:

No. Not a bit, not a bit.
Not a bit, not a bit, not a bit, not a bit in the world.

But he was sayin' he might be comin' home.

SON:

Home?
When?

DADDA:

Eh, Thursday …

SON:

This Thursday?

DADDA:

Eh? That's what he said.

SON:

Ya mean like today, like?!

DADDA:

Is today Thursday?

SON:

Well Jesus, yesterday was Wednesday!

DADDA:

Oh right, today then, today …

SON:

Today?!

DADDA:

Well, that's what he said.

SON:

Did he say he was comin' home – home?

Or did he just say he was comin' home ...

DADDA:

Eh, just said he was comin' home ...

* * *

SON: [directly to audience]

Like I'm sittin' here – waiting on the storm.
[hissed] Jesus Maneen ...
A spanner in the works – an accident waitin' to happen.
And as sure as oil floats on water –
A cold wind blows wherever Maneen goes.

Everytime he comes home – it's always something else!
I ask meself – what's it gonna be this time ...

* * *

[MANEEN and DADDA in car – MANEEN is driving – DADDA is not engaging with MANEEN – but rather he's deep in his own thoughts]

DADDA:

Great to have ya home, Maneen! Great to have ye home!

MANEEN: *[looking in wonder at new developments]*
>Jesus the city is boomin', Dad.
>Feel it the second, ya step off the plane.
>You can smell the money in the air.
>Like a boom town in a gold rush …

DADDA: *[directly to audience – internal thoughts]*
>Ah, yes, I love when Maneen come home.
>A bit of spark about the place …

MANEEN:
>That new hotel over on the quay?
>'Tis like Las Vegas.
>And the apartments – poppin' up all over the place,
>can hardly see the sky for the cranes.

DADDA: *[directly to audience – internal thoughts]*
>Don't get me wrong – I love the two lads.
>But they're chalk and cheese.
>And Jesus when they get together –
>they're like a bag a' cats …

MANEEN:
>That's fine job they done on Patrick Street.
>The new lights look shite!
>La, more apartments.
>Big changes – the cafes, shops, new cars, cappuccino.
>Ya can smell the money in this town.

DADDA: *[directly to audience – internal thoughts]*
>Maybe it's me – I don't know?
>But I spent me life trying to keep peace between the two of
>them.

MANEEN:
>Did ya talk to Son, Dad?

DADDA: *[directly to audience – internal thoughts]*
>And if there's one thing that I've learned it's,
>when two elephants go to war –
>'tis the grass gets trampled.
>And I've learned to stay well outa' their way …

MANEEN:
>Dad?!

DADDA: *[snapped away from internal thoughts]*
>What? Eh, sorry? What were you sayin'?

MANEEN:
>Just askin' – did ya talk to Son?

DADDA:
>About what?

MANEEN:
>About the estate agent – and sellin' the place?

DADDA: *[dismissive]*
>Sellin' the place? No, I did not!

* * *

DADDA: *[shouts to SON in the chicken shed]*
>Hoi! Son!
>[whistle as if calling a dog]
>Maneen's home!
>Bring in his bags outa' the car there – will ya!

[SON arrives long-armed as if carrying bags]

SON:

Hey Maneen! Good to see you!
Will ya be stayin' long?

MANEEN:

Jesus, I'm just in the door – and he's askin' me when I'm goin'
back?

SON: *[defensive splutter]*
Ah, well now I didn't mean it that …

DADDA: *[to SON]*
Look, make yer self useful there,
an' put on the kettle or somethin', will ya!

SON:

Eh, right Dadda …

*[DADDA shouts a string of orders at SON – sending him this way and
that around the stage doing jobs for MANEEN]*

MANEEN: *[to DADDA]*
Jesus I'm starving' from all the travel.

SON:

I'll throw a few eggs into the pan there for you, Maneen.

DADDA: *[to SON]*
Don't mind yer aul' eggs,
Throw on the sausages as well – will ya!

SON:

The Sunday mornin' sausages, Dadda?

DADDA: *[to SON]*

'Tisn't every day that Maneen be comin' home. Hah!
Fill up the pan, for Christ's sake, Son! Fill up the pan!
[To MANEEN] Sit down there Maneen!

[SON is sent this way and that as DADDA and MANEEN shout various orders at him]

DADDA:

Is the kettle boiled, Son!

SON: *[SON changes direction and heads across the stage]*

Eh, right Dadda, right!

MANEEN:

How're them sausages comin' on, Son?

SON: *[SON changes direction and heads across the stage]*

On the way now, Maneen!

DADDA:

Son! Clear off the table there while yer at it, will ya?!

SON: *[SON changes direction and heads across the stage]*

Straight away, Dadda!

DADDA:

Son throw his bags down to the room, like a good lad …

* * *

[SON leads MANEEN down stage as if carrying the bags – looking towards the audience as if facing bunk bed]

MANEEN:

> Hey! Hey! Hey! Who's been sleepin' in my bed?

SON:

> Your bed?

MANEEN:

> You can throw the bags up on top a' me bunk there!

SON: [confused]

> But the top bunk's my bunk?

MANEEN:

> You rob me grave as quick? would ya!

SON:

> Well what bunk do you want?

MANEEN:

> Want?! Want don't come into it, Sonny boy!
> The top bunk is my bunk!
> Was then, is now and ever shall be my bunk!

SON:

> Look, for a quiet life – whatever you say, whatever you say …

MANEEN:

> But d'ya know, Son?

SON:

> What now, Maneen?

MANEEN:

> I think I'll sleep in the bottom bunk for tonight
> seeing as it's made up an all.
> We can change around tomorrow.

SON:

Fair enough Maneen – fair enough ...

* * *

[Morning – SON working on car. MANEEN arrives, walks around him a number of times. SON looks up from his work bemused – Maybe SON is lying on the ground as if fixing a car underneath. MANEEN is physically talking down to him]

SON:

You decided to get outa' bed !?

MANEEN:

Yer some man to strip down a car all the same.

SON: *[preoccupied with work]*

MANEEN:

Like Dad says ...

SON: *[preoccupied with work]*

MANEEN:

Brain of a mechanic – hands of a surgeon ...

SON: *[preoccupied with work]*

MANEEN:

Yer hard at it?!

SON: *[Gets to his feet.]*
Tippin' away, Maneen. Tippin' away ...
See that Ford over there?

MANEEN:

> Not in bad nick for a '92 …

SON:

> That car might look perfect.
> But if you examine it closely,
> you'll find one hairline crack on the right hand indicator lens.
> And that little crack – tells story …
>
> Connected with a woman – out the Dublin Road.
> Car hit the bank and –
> [horizontal clap]
> flat down on top of the ditch.
> Made shit of the chassis – A total right off!

MANEEN:

> And the woman?

SON:

> Power walkin'!
> And I'm tellin' ya when a woman doin' ten miles an hour goin'
> this way,
> connects with a car doin' eighty goin' that way –
> there's only one outcome … *[vertical clap]*

MANEEN:

> Jesus …

SON:

> Stone dead!
> Said she was out tryin' to walk off a' bit a weight for her
> daughter's weddin'.
> Yer not gonna believe this –
> but when they weighed her remains at the undertaker's –
> she'd lost three stone in the impact.

MANEEN:

>The fright, was it?

SON:

>Not at all!
>There was bits of her body blown all over the road!
>Sur' there were scrapin' up dead hedgehogs, rabbits and vermin for a hundred yards – just to have somethin' to put inta' the coffin.
>Made total shit of her!
>Funny thing is –
>not a scratch on the car – hah?!
>The only giveaway when that car came into the yard here – was me chickens.

MANEEN:

>Yer chickens?

SON:

>Chalk it down! Went berserk!
>So they did.
>A feeding frenzy – pickin' her brains offa' the front bumper there …

MANEEN: [disgusted]

>Ah, Jezus, Son …

SON:

>Tellin' ya, ya come across some fairly strange things in this game …

MANEEN:

>But yer busy all the time, ya are?

SON:

Ah, the spare parts game is changin'–
'tis all new cars on the road these days …
I mean Jesus, keepin' bangers goin' was always my bread and
butter.

MANEEN:

Yer managing to keep Dad's aul' banger on the road?

SON:

I do, I do, I do, I keep her tickin' over alright.

'Tis more my car now – Dadda don't drive that much no
more?

MANEEN:

*[a put-down undermining his ability as a mechanic / maybe sexual
undertones]*
The eh, clutch is a bit soft on her.

SON:

The clutch?

MANEEN:

Only a small thing like –
but I noticed it last night drivin' down from the airport.
The clutch – a bit soft like.

SON:

You drove down from the airport?!

MANEEN:

Sur' as you say – Dadda don't drive that much.

SON:

>Old cars – are like old dogs …
>only has one master – ya know what I mean!
>'Cause that clutch is – perfectly adjusted –
>*[Implying MANEEN is too big for his boots]*

>maybe 'tis your boots are a bit too heavy.

MANEEN: *[sparring in some nostalgic emotional duelling]*

>Maybe yer right, maybe yer right…
>But, Dad was sayin' 'twas probably all your freewheelin' –
>down to Martina Foley like.
>*[sexual implication]*
>The aul' freewheelin' can be very heavy on the aul' clutch, ya
>know…

SON: *[SON refuses to be drawn into Maneen's game – and returns to work]*

>… ya think so, do ya?

MANEEN:

>That's what Dad was sayin'.
>Lot a' memories wrapped up in this yard, all the same?
>The aul' cowboys and Indians …
>Isn't that right – Cochise …

[SON reacts to being called Cochise]

SON:

>And what about the hide and seek!
>The aul' chicken shed is still standin'…

MANEEN: *[The mention of Chicken Shed brings a look of chill/fear to MANEEN's face]*

[MANEEN is transported back to the past when he was a child – while SON remains detached as if commentating on what is unfolding – MANEEN and SON are standing down stage – delivering directly to audience]

SON: *[cont'd.]*
>   The aul' chicken shed …
>   …the one place I get a bit of peace and quiet.
>   I be hidin' and you be seekin',
>   that right Maneen?

MANEEN: *[childlike counting - hands over eyes – hide and seek]*
>   96, 97, 98, 99, One hundred!
>   Ok Son, ready or not here I come!

SON:
>   You're too small to climb up onto the roof of the chicken shed
>   and I'm up there balmin' out in the sun …

MANEEN: *[childlike]*
>   I know you're in there, come out, Son …

SON:
>   On the roof of the chicken shed – safe as houses, lookin'
>   down.
>   A birds-eye view.
>   Looking down on you scurrying up and down the yard –
>   and ya rootin' around behind old cars.

MANEEN: *[childlike]*
>   Come out, Son, I know you're in there …

Son:
>   Watchin' ya dartin' in and out of the tool shed –
>   An' around the back of the diesel tank.

MANEEN: *[childlike]*
>Son? Son? Where are ya, Son?

SON:
>And I'm lookin' down.
>You're at the chicken shed door and I can hear you …

[SFX: fade up – haunting, music box music]
[The mood gradually changes from two children playing to something far more sinister.]
MANEEN:
>Mammy?
>What ya doin' in the chicken shed, Mammy?
>Mammy?
>Did ya see Son?
>Did ya see Son, Mammy?
>Ya lookin' for eggs?
>Did ya see Son, Mam?

SON:
>And I'm up here lookin' down,
>sayin' nothin' and smilin'.

MANEEN: *[to MAMMY – he is slightly transfixed]*
>That's an amazin' trick?
>Where did ya learn that, Mammy!
>That's an amazin' trick …
>Mammy? Did ya see Son, Mammy?

SON:
>The curiosity is getting the better of me.
>But you were always the sly one Maneen.
>I remember thinkin' it was just a trick to entice me down from me hiding place …

MANEEN: *[looking at MAMMY's feet]*
>   Where did ya learn that trick, Mammy – that's a brilliant trick!
>   Just to be floatin' there off the ground.
>   I can see right under your feet, Mam.
>   That's amazin'…

[MANEEN's appearance changes to a look of amazement]
>   Son! Son! Come out wherever you are!
>   Look at Mammy!
>   She's inside the chicken shed,
>   floatin' in the air.

SON:
>   But curiosity gets the better of me.
>   Slid down off the side of the chicken shed roof and I …

[He stops in his tracks – also looks on in amazement.]
>   I can't believe me eyes …

MANEEN: *[childlike]*
>   See? What did I tell ya? What did I tell ya, Son?
>   She's floatin' in the air…

SON: *[disbelief – wonder]*
>   And I'm just standin' there lookin' in …
>   Can't believe what I'm seeing?
>   My mother, she's floatin' there in mid–air.
>   Maneen is pushin' her this way and that …
>   And I'm lookin' at her feet – about six inches off the ground.
>   Just floatin' there …

MANEEN:
>   That's amazin'…

SON: *[There's a gradual realisation that MAMMY has committed suicide.]*
>   And all I can hear is the creakin' of a rope.
>   Stretchin' on the rafters as she's swingin' there …

Swingin' by a rope to her neck…
[panic] Jesus, Maneen, hold her up! Hold her up, will ya!

MANEEN: [direct to audience]
And I'm holding on to me Mam, I'm holding on to her!

SON:
And I'm strugglin' with the rope.

MANEEN:
Little hands tryin' to hold her steady!

SON:
Rope is slippin' – Ah, Jesus Maneen, will ya hold her!

MANEEN:
I'm holdin' her!

SON:
Skinnin' me knuckles!

MANEEN:
She swingin' this way and that – and I'm holdin' on for life!

SON:
Hold her, Maneen! Jesus Christ, hold her!

MANEEN:
I'm holdin' her, Son! Hurry will ya!

SON:
Rope slips – And Mammy…

MANEEN:
My mother falls like a sack a' chicken feed …

SON:

> … a dead weight to the ground.

MANEEN:

> Still holdin' on – her eyes bulgin'.

SON:

> And you're pinned to the ground – by the weight of my dead mother's body.

MANEEN:

> And I'm cryin', and holdin' and pressed into the straw, and the filth …

* * *

DADDA: *[directly to audience]*

> Two things crossed my mind,
> when I saw her lying there that day.
> Don't get me wrong now – I loved her.
> But hand on heart – I can't say I ever understood her.
> Maybe it was me – I don't know.
> But she was like a dark cloud on a sunny day.
> Always at war with herself.
>
> I remember it like it were yesterday.
> I was out. Out the yard – under a Cortina.
> Could hear the young fellas.
> Runnin' 'round the place – a rootin' and a hootin'.
> Playin' hide and seek – or something.
>
> And then – nothin'.
> Not a sound.
> And when them two young fellas go silent –

You can bet yer bottom dollar – there's something wrong.
So I down tools.
Make my way to the chicken shed door.
Maneen? Maneen's pinned there to the ground – whimperin'.
Son standing there holding the rope – sobbin'.

Jesus … [whispered]
She's lyin' there – face contorted.

And two things cross me mind.

Thank Christ – she's at peace at last.
And, who's gonna help me rear the two young fellas.

[SON and MANEEN back to present]

SON:

Remember the aul' hide and seek, Maneen?
I be hidin' and you be seekin' isn't that right?
And the chicken shed?!

MANEEN:

Never liked that chicken shed.

SON:

It's the one place I always get a bit a' peace and quiet.

MANEEN:

Look, Son.
for the past while –
I spent a fair share a' me time thinkin' about this place …

SON:

This place?

MANEEN:

Plannin' for our future like?!

SON:

Our future?

MANEEN:

Well, the price a' property's gone bananas in this town.
It's not gonna stay that way for ever …

SON:

What's that gotta do with – our future?

MANEEN:

All ya has to do is look around ya …
I mean Jesus –
There's car parts there that'll never see the road again.
Not many people comin' in here lookin' for a rusty bonnet off
a' Vauxhall Viva.

SON:

But sur' 'tis the day I throw it out,
is the day someone'll come lookin' for it …

MANEEN:

Well, maybe it's time ya thought of sellin' the place …

SON:

What're ya talkin' about!

MANEEN:

Just sayin' like …
Sur' look you said it yerself – them days are gone …

SON:

>Didn't say they were gone!
>Just that they were changin'–
>That's all!

MANEEN:

>The whole world is changin' –
>I mean, even if ya didn't want to sell.
>Throw up a half dozen houses …

SON:

>But sur' haven't we got a house …

MANEEN:

>We could develop the place ourselves.

SON:

>What's this *we* business!

MANEEN:

>I'm only thinkin' about our future.
>Yer sittin' on a fortune here …

SON:

>What about my car parts?

MANEEN:

>What about 'em!
>Look, there's two types a people in this world –
>them that works for money – and –
>them that makes money work for them!

SON: *[processing]*

>There's three types –
>'cause there's people like me – who don't think about money –
>But just likes what they're doing …

MANEEN:

>Think what the place is worth?!

SON:

>It's only worth something if ya sell it!

MANEEN:

>Exactly! That's my point!
>In fast! Quick kill! Make a buck!
>That's how it's done!

SON:

>But it's not for sale!

MANEEN:

>How do ya mean it's not for sale?!
>Do ya have any idea what a place like this is worth?

SON:

>It don't matter what it's worth! Not for sale!

MANEEN:

>Jesus Christ,
>You'd want to wake up and smell the coffee beans, Son!

SON:

>What coffee beans!??
>I'm a bread and jam man!
>And listen! My name - is not - Son!

MANEEN:

>You're livin' in a fuckin' time warp, boy!
>I mean Jesus, look around ya! Look around ya!
>The town's explodin' with development –
>And you're here …

Tearin' a door offa Renault 4…
Up to your neck in chicken shit. – fuck's sake …

SON:

You can take them dollar signs outa yer eyes, right quick now,
Maneen!

MANEEN:

I mean Jesus …

SON: [SON *heads to chicken shed.*]
I've no more to say on the matter …
End a' story!

MANEEN:

For Christ's sake!
Come back! I'm talkin' to ya!

* * *

[*Scene notes – DADDA is blind to all of MANEEN's manoeuvrings.
DADDA's only preoccupation is his bingo. On the other hand we see
MANEEN change from a person who is disillusioned in London to a
person who recognises an opportunity in Ireland.*]

DADDA:

You were out talkin' to himself?

MANEEN:

Chickens and car parts.
Jesus! May as well be talkin' to the wall!
I dunno, Dadda – maybe you could say something to him.

DADDA:

And say what?

MANEEN:

Talk sense to him – about sellin' the place.

DADDA:

He have his own way of doing things – yer brother!

MANEEN:

My half-brother!

DADDA:

Jesus you're not on about that old chestnut again – are ya!

MANEEN:

It's true, Dadda – and you know it!
We're sittin' on a fortune –
And he's out there pullin' a door off a fuckin' Renault 4!
I mean Jesus! What the fuck is that about!

DADDA:

Ah, Son likes the physical work …

MANEEN:

God sake, Dadda – the only muscle he need to use these days
is his brain.

DADDA:

He likes doin' things the way they've always been done.

MANEEN:

You heard what the estate agent said.

DADDA:

Son seems happy enough the way things are.

MANEEN:

What do being happy have to do with anything! Hah!?
[hissed] Jezus …

[Uncomfortable silence – then DADDA breaks the ice.]

DADDA: *[Obviously not as concerned as MANEEN]*
When you were out talkin' to Son –
Did he eh, mention anything about the bingo?

MANEEN:

No nothin' about the bingo!

DADDA:

Nothin' about droppin me down to the hall, or nothin'?

MANEEN:

No …

DADDA:

I missed me lucky book last week over him.
Missed the shaggin' jackpot!
Too busy up talkin' to his chickens he was …

MANEEN: *[He realises this is an opportunity to make his case to DADDA.]*
Sur' look – I could drop ya down to the bingo – if ya want?

DADDA:

Ya wouldn't mind?

MANEEN:

    Sur' I'm only twiddlin' me thumbs – getting' in the way
    around here.
    If ya like we can go for a pint after?

DADDA:

    Jesus – d'ya know? That'd be great! I'd love that.
    What about Son? Will I give him a shout?

MANEEN:

    He's happy out talkin' to his chickens – give him the night off.

DADDA:

    The night off?

MANEEN:

    I wouldn't mind a bit of a chat with ya –
    on yer own like.

DADDA: *[slightly intrigued]*

    Right –
    We will then – we will.
    We'll give him the night off …

* * *

SON: *[directly to audience – reflective – slow logical build]*

    I don't know …
    Everythin's changed?!
    Everythin's changed.
    I always lived in me small brother's shadow –
    and that don't bother me.
    Maneen's as bright as a button.
    Lighten up a room, he would.

That's the way he is – and that don't bother me.

Maneen and Dadda? Like peas in a pod.
Always feeding off each other, bouncing off each other,
rising each other.
And why wouldn't they be – they are son and father,
and that don't bother me –
'cause blood will always be thicker than water.

But Jesus – when he cleared off to London ten years ago,
Dadda had to learn to make do with me.
Forced out a' the shadow and into the spotlight – I was.
An' Dadda? It took him time now mind, but he learned.
He learned to feed off me, to bounce off me, live off me,
and we found our rhythm.

And no doubt every time himself 'd come home for the
holidays,
It'd throw everythin' in the air.
But when he'd go back, it'd all settle down again.

But, last week, when Maneen walked back in that door there,
'twas different!
'Twas like? 'Twas like he was home.
'Twas like he'd just stepped out and stepped back in again!
Nothin' changed!
Only thing that's changed around here, is me …
An' fuck-it! I'm not steppin' back into the shadows for no one.
Everythin's changed!
Everythin's changed, cause nothin's changed!
Nothin's changed!
An' Jesus – that's what bothers me!

* * *

[Enter MANEEN and DADDA after bingo – they are in high spirits. SON is clearly not happy.]

DADDA:

Somethin' botherin' ya, Son?

SON:

Only one thing botherin' me, Dadda …

DADDA:

What's that?

SON:

Everythin'!

DADDA:

Hah?

SON:

You never called me down for to drive ya to the bingo this evenin'!

DADDA:

Didn't want to be disturbin' ya.

SON:

Disturbin' me?!

MANEEN: *[sarcastic]*

Y'know – your bedtime chat with your chickens.

SON: [dismissing MANEEN with a glare – SON talks to DADDA]
Every Tuesday night for the past 10 year I drives ya down to the bingo –
you'd no problem disturbin' me then!?

MANEEN:
Look-it! I drove him down this evenin',
save ya the trouble, like.

DADDA:
'Tisn't like ya missed much, Son.
Sur' all you'd be doin' is waitin' in the car for me
to come out again …

MANEEN:
Just thought we'd give ya the night off …

SON: [directly to DADDA]
Night off!?

MANEEN:
Yeah, a night off!

SON: [glares at MANEEN – continues talking to DADDA]
Did it ever cross yer mind that maybe –
I enjoys drivin' down to the bingo!
And that maybe I enjoys callin' to Foley's to get the messages.
And that I enjoys havin' me bit of a chat with Martina Foley.

Did it ever cross yer mind Dadda, that –
Tuesday might be as much my night out as it is yours!

DADDA: [confused look]

MANEEN:

    Sur' look, we didn't even go to the bingo – anyhow!

SON: [disbelief]

    Didn't go to the bingo?

DADDA:

    Eh? No, Son? Eh, not tonight …

SON: [disbelief]

    Where did ye go – so?!

MANEEN: [goading SON]

    Went for a few pints instead …

SON: [disbelief]

    Pints?

DADDA:

    Ya know? Maneen bein' home an' all?
    Just a few pints …

SON:

    A few pints?!

DADDA:

    Look, me heart wasn't in the bingo after losin' out to the
    jackpot last week –
    and then Maneen being home – an' all – an' …

SON:

    Ye went for a few pints?

MANEEN:

>   Yeah a few fuckin' pints! Jesus!
>   Is there an echo in this room or what!

SON:

>   Why didn't ye bring me with ye?

MANEEN:

>   'Tis like the fuckin' Spanish Inquisition with ya!
>   Look-it! You were up talkin' to yer chickens!
>
>   I offered to drive Dadda down to the bingo!
>   And on the way there we decided to go for a few pints instead!
>   Alright! Alright?

* * *

[Next evening – SON is out in yard working on car – enter DADDA]

DADDA:

>   Mornin', Son?

SON: *[minimal acknowledgement of DADDA – subdued but builds in frustration]*

>   Dadda …

DADDA:

>   Said – I'd come down – talk to ya.

[SON does not answer]

DADDA:

>   Look, I'm sorry about last night.

You know, the bingo an' all.
It won't happen again …

SON:

'Tis more than the bingo, Dadda. And you know it …
Ever since he come back, he struttin' around the place –
like cock-of-the-walk!
And you know it, Dadda! You know it damned well!

DADDA:

Ah now, Son!

SON:

Don't, ah now Son, me, Dadda!

DADDA:

Maneen just need time to settle in, that's all …

SON:

Settle in! What I want to know is?
When is he goin' back!

DADDA:

Ah, sur' Christ's sake, Son.
You know Maneen?

SON:

I know him too well! And I can't take no more of him!
Out there tellin' me we should sell the place.
Sell the place! I mean what fuckin' planet is he on!?

DADDA:

You know him as well as I do!

SON:

Look, you and Maneen have always been like that, la!
[two fingers held together]

And that don't bother me!
But Jesus Christ - in all honesty, Dadda,
if yer two sons turned out like him –
this place would be well and truly fucked!
An' you know that! An' I can't take much more of it!

DADDA:

Just listen to me - listen to me now!

SON:

I spend me life listenin' to ya!
It's about time that someone listened to me for a change!
Do anyone care what I think!

DADDA:

I care.
I fuckin' care for you, Son – always have!

SON:

Yeah well it don't fuckin' feel like that!

DADDA:

Yeah well I fuckin' well do!

[strained/cold silence]

DADDA:

Suppose 'tis a bit like, like Luke?

SON:

Luke?
Who the fuck is Luke?

DADDA:

    St Luke …
    In the gospel.
    The Prodigal Son, like?

SON:

    Prodigal Son?!

DADDA:

    I mean Jesus, I care for the both of ye.
    But, I suppose – it's only natural –
    that there's always –
    always a special place in the heart for the one that's away?

SON:

    Well that's no good to the one who stays behind breakin' his
    fuckin' balls!

DADDA:

    I'm not sayin' 'tis right!

SON:

    Damned right it's not right!

DADDA:

    It like the jockey,
    and he winnin' the race,
    and he spurring and whipping the winning horse!
    I mean Jesus you'd have to ask yerself, why?!
    Well I'll tell ya why!

    There's no point flakin' the also rans! That's why!
    And Maneen? Maneen is an also ran!
    Just give him time, Son! That's all I'm askin'!
    Just give him time!

SON:

Time? [whisper] Fuck's sake!
I saw him headin' down town again in the car …

DADDA:

And what about it?!

SON:

Soft clutch! I'll give him soft clutch!
He's worn a track from the yard all the way into Patrick's
Street.
In an' out, in an out, in an out every fuckin' day.
[hah?] Sur' that's pure and simple madness, Dadda!

DADDA:

Maybe it'd be no harm if you went down town yourself,
once in a while …

SON:

What'd be drawin' me down town!?

DADDA:

People, Son! People yer own age!
Did I hear ya say –
There was an aul' concert tonight or somethin'?

SON:

Oh, that!?
Martina Foley was sayin' something about Daniel O'Donnell.

DADDA:

There ya go …

SON:

Sur' I've no interest in seeing Daniel O'fuckin' Donnell!
Christ's sake …

DADDA:

Ya might even enjoy yerself.
Couldn't ya go down and ask Martina Foley to go in along
with ya?

SON:

Martina Foley?
Where ya getting' Martina Foley from!?

DADDA:

For the company, like …

SON: *[realising the possibility]*
Martina Foley and me?
Naw? Naw? Naw?
No way …

DADDA:

Why? Did ya ask her, or somethin'?

SON:

Course I didn't ask her!
She'd have no interest in someone like me.

DADDA:

What are ya sayin'!
Think about it, Son? Think about it?

SON:

Naw?/[or confused look]

DADDA:

I'm tellin' ya …

SON:

Sayin' me, Dadda?
Me and Martina Foley?

DADDA:

Bingo!

SON:

Naw?

DADDA:

… a blind man could see the manoeuvring.
Mrs Foley and her,
[mimic MRS FOLEY] Martina! Martina!
An' the way she be out to you every time you set foot inside
the shop.

SON:

Think so, Dadda?

DADDA:

Think so? I know so!
Go ask her, Son!

SON:

Me and Martina Foley?

DADDA:

Just go ask her will ya …

SON:

Me and Martina?
D'ya know - I might then.
I might go down an' ask her to come down town with me.
Just for the company, like …

DADDA:

    Too right, you might!

SON: [*A sense of excitement building with the prospect of asking* MARTINA *on a date*]

    Bring her down a few eggs while I'm at it. So I might …

DADDA:

    No might about it, Son! Just go an' do it will ya!
    Good lad, Son. Good lad …

* * *

[SON *removes dirty overalls as he recites monologue – he's wearing a clean white shirt – and black trousers*]

SON: [*directly to audience*]

    Throw on the shirt.
    Wet back the hair.
    Give the boots a rub a' the cloth.

    Jeezuz! Maneen's gone with the car?!
    So I strike off down to Foley's, on foot.
    Hobnail boots liftin' dust and knockin' sparks off the road.
    And I'm stridin' along the bent and buckley,
    like I'm freewheelin'.
    Driven on by every muscle, bone and sinew in my body.
    Driven on by life …
    Driven on to meet Martina …

    Tinkle–tinkle–tinkle!
    And – How're ya Mrs Foley!

[Transition: Maneen to Mrs Foley]

Mrs Foley:

>   Well Sonny, wouldn't expect to see you here on a Thursday.
>   Show us? G've us a look of you, Sonny?
>   *[Son is bashful because of the praise of his clean clothes]*
>   You're all dressed up!
>   Is it a funeral you're goin' to?

Son:

>   [laugh] A funeral? Eh, no, Mrs Foley. No!
>   Eh, I'm eh, just wonderin', eh?
>   Is Martina inside at all?

Mrs Foley:

>   Martina?
>   No, Martina's gone.

Son:

>   Gone, Mrs Foley?

Mrs Foley:

>   She gone about a half an hour.

Son:

>   Gone where?

Mrs Foley:

>   Your brother! Your brother Maneen.

Son: *[confused]*

>   Maneen? Mrs Foley?

Mrs Foley:

>   In to see Daniel O'Donnell, they're gone!

SON:

> [SON *is obviously upset by this news*]
> Daniel O'Donnell? Mrs Foley?

MRS FOLEY:

> Will I give Martina a message for you?
> Or, can I do anythin' for ya meself?

SON: [*devastated*]

> Errah, no, Mrs Foley – No.
> I just, eh, got a few eggs here –
> I just wanted to drop off for eh, Mr Foley's breakfast …

MRS FOLEY:

> Eggs?
> Well that's very thoughtful of you?
> Aren't the two a' ye great lads now, all the same.

SON:

> Two of us, Mrs Foley?

MRS FOLEY:

> Yourself bringin' us down these lovely fresh eggs,
> and yer brother, Maneen bringin' down a chicken.

SON:

> A chicken, Mrs Foley?

MRS FOLEY:

> Didn't Maneen bring us down a present of a lovely fresh
> chicken, plucked and ready for the pot.

SON: [*shocked*]

> No! Not Reddy!?

MRS FOLEY:

'Twas now! Perfectly plucked, cleaned out and ready for the pot!

SON:

No, Mrs Foley! Don't tell me 'twas Reddy?

MRS FOLEY:

'Twas ...

SON:

No not Reddy!
Don't say 'twas Reddy!

MRS FOLEY:

'Twas ready. Plucked and ready for the ...

SON: [directly to audience]

An' I'm standin' there in a daze.
Mrs Foley's words - like poisoned flies.
Spiralling around the Vapona,
droppin' down one-by-one dead in front of me eyes.
She's sayin' something about my father,
And him being such a great man for rearing two such fine sons all on his own.

It's like I'm chokin' from the Vapona and the smell a' the shop.
I make for the door and air.
I can hear Mrs Foley ...

MRS FOLEY:

Eh, Sonny? Are you okay Sonny? Sonny?
Will I give Martina a message for you ...

SON:

Tinkle–tinkle–tinkle. Shop door close behind me.

* * *

[Transition: MRS FOLEY to MANEEN]

MANEEN :

The second Martina Foley sat into the car,
I knew what I was doing wasn't right.
Don't get me wrong, I love me brother,
but it crossed my mind that what I was doin' –
was out a' pure spite.

And it's only true to say –
when we saw the House Full sign on the door a' the concert,
it was a relief in a funny sort of way.

But Martina suggested, seeing as we were down town we
should go for a drink.
Why not, says I. So we went on a mini–tour …
Canty's, Counihan's, Long Valley, Hi-B.

And I'll say one thing for Martina Foley,
by Christ can she talk.
Talk for Ireland so she would.
But, we were having a laugh,
and what started out as an act of spite,
was shaping up to being – a fairly good night.

* * *

[SON enters kitchen deranged with anger and disappointment]

DADDA:

    Jez, I thought you were gone down town, Son.
    Did ya forget something?

SON:

    Forgot nothin'!

DADDA:

    What about Martina Foley and the concert?

SON:

    He killed her!

DADDA:

    Hah?

SON:

    He killed her, Dadda!

DADDA:

    Who killed her?

SON:

    Maneen did!

DADDA: *[shock]*

    Maneen killed Martina Foley?!

SON:

    Ah Jesus, no!
    Maneen killed Reddy!

DADDA:

    Reddy who!

SON:

Reddy! My new chicken, the one I was tellin' ya about.

DADDA: *[pause for recollection]*

The mechanic?

SON:

Plucked and cleaned for the pot – he had her!

DADDA:

Well, thank Christ -'twas only one a' yer chickens!
I thought 'twas Martina Foley he was after killing!

SON: *[becoming more upset]*

He just went up there to the yard, picked out my Reddy and
murdered her! Murdered her in cold blood, Dadda!

DADDA:

Ah, now Son, I know what he did was way outa order.
But, ya can't really call it murder! I mean Jesus,
a chicken's a chicken …

SON:

He did it for spite, Dadda!

DADDA:

Ah, for Christ's sake, Son – don't be like that....

SON:

Don't be like what! Like what!
He went down to Martina Foley!
Down to Martina!
She was waitin' for me you – said it yerself!
He had the pick a' London,
and he goes down to Martina Foley!

He've no interest in her Dadda!
He've no interest in her ...

DADDA:

Ah, Son for Christ's sake, come back an' sit down will ya!
Ah, come on Son...

SON:

No more Dadda! No more!

* * *

MANEEN:

Canty's, Counihan's, Long Valley, Hi-B.
But with a half a gallon inside me –
and four or five short ones on top of it,
decided best to get the car home –
not to go too far over the limit.

Now maybe it was me, or maybe it was she?
But as we making our way along Drawbridge Street,
the next thing I know?
Whamo! Me back's to a door.
And like a lizard – her tongue is darting in and out
and slithering all over inside me mouth.

And like on autopilot,
found myself thrown down on the back seat of the car –
and Martina Foley has her knickers off,
her dress pulled up and she's straddling me.
Up and down! Up and down! Up and down!
Ridin' me like a jockey.

Up and down!

Up and down!
Up and down …
And as she moves from canter, to trot, to gallop –
she starts to talk.
She talks about her first boyfriend, her mother, her father, her
brother's wife, her favourite pair of shoes and her first day at
school.
She talks about the price of sugar and two stone of potatoes.
She talks about Hollywood.
She says there's a dark side to Johnny Depp,
George Clooney could do with a bit a colour in his hair,
and Brad Pitt's a shit.
She talks about the value of Dunnes Stores,
says Centra is friendlier,
And Tesco? Don't get me started on Tesco?

And she's riding me there on the back seat of the car,
and the stream of utter scutter – about that and this,
spewin' from her flappin' lips.

It crosses my mind, that maybe,
maybe Martina's need to talk is only matched by my need to
make love,
and I'm makin' love and she's talking
and that seems like a fair deal to me.

So she talks, and talks, and talks …
Up and down, up and down, up and down.
Talk for Ireland so she would.
I close my eyes, throws back my head and think to meself –
Jesus –
Isn't love a funny old game?

And, God …
It's great to be home all the same!

[next morning – MANEEN arrives into kitchen]

DADDA: [cold]
    I suppose you're proud of yerself!

MANEEN: [defensive]
    What am I after doin' now.

DADDA:
    You know damned well what yer after doin'!

MANEEN:
    Oh, the chicken..!?
    Christ's sake! It was only a bit of a joke!

DADDA:
    I'm not talkin' about chicken!
    I'm talkin' about you goin' down to Martina Foley's and …

MANEEN:
    Jesus, I just asked the girl out! Where's the sin in that!

DADDA:
    Don't play the fuckin' eejit with me, Maneen!
    I tellin' ya straight – go out there and talk to him!

MANEEN:
    About what?

DADDA:
    Maneen!?
    Go out and talk to him – now!

SECOND CITY TRILOGY

MANEEN:
Jesus Christ …

* * *

[Yard – Son working on car]

MANEEN:
Son?!

SON: *[ignoring MANEEN]*

MANEEN:
Not a bad day …

SON: *[ignoring MANEEN]*

MANEEN:
Look the aul' fella said I should come down – talk to ya.

SON: *[ignoring MANEEN]*

MANEEN:
I know what I did last night was way outa' order.

SON: *[dismissive]*

MANEEN:
'Twas just a bit of a joke – gone wrong, that's all …

[Son looks at MANEEN]

MANEEN:

Just want things to go back to the way that they were, between you and me – like …

SON:

Well I don't want things to go back to the way they were between you and me – like!

MANEEN:

Well that's a start, at least we're talking.

SON:

I've nothin' to say to you, Maneen.

Found a knickers in the back seat a' the car.
Threw it into the bin if yer lookin' for it!

MANEEN:

Ah, Jesus, look sorry about Martina Foley.
I mean, the last thing I had in my mind was upsetting you.
Ya know?

SON:

You've a funny way of not upsettin' people.

MANEEN:

Jesus, I came home with a head full of ideas …

SON:

Yeah, well – who asked ya for yer ideas!

MANEEN:

That's more of it!
Everytime I open my mouth,
I only get slapped down – by you!
I mean – with the greatest respect …

SON:

> Greatest respect?!
> Anyone who has to say, with the greatest respect –
> usually have no respect at all!

MANEEN:

> Look, you and Dadda?
> Ye're livin' in a goldfish bowl!
> Just swimmin' round and round in circles.
> I'm only thinkin' of what's best for all of us,
> the big picture …

SON:

> What big picture?!

MANEEN:

> I said it before – there's two kinds a' people in this world,
> Them that works for money,
> and them that make money work for them …

SON:

> No! There's three kinds,
> 'cause, there's fellas like me,
> fellas who couldn't give a fuck about money –
> but loves what they do …

[enter DADDA]

MANEEN:

> Yeah well this isn't all about you - ya know!

[SON looks to DADDA]

MANEEN:

Tell him, Dad.

[DADDA *looks confused/cornered*]

Tell him about the estate agent …

SON:

Estate agent!?

MANEEN:

Tell him what this place worth, Dad?!

[DADDA *caught for words*]

SON:

What estate agent?

DADDA:

Well eh, there was a fella came up, like?
A friend a' Maneen's and …

MANEEN:

Tell him what he said!

SON:

You had an estate agent up here!?

DADDA:

You know – a friend a' Maneen's?
For a quiet life I just said he could, take a look of the place …

SON:

Take a look of the place?

DADDA:

You know – for a quiet life – like.

SON:

Without tellin' me?

MANEEN:

Tell him how much the place is worth, Dad!

DADDA:

He just threw a ball park figure? That's all …

SON:

Ball park me bollocks!

MANEEN:

Look you can stay buried up to yer balls in axle grease for the
rest of yer life for all I care!
But if the place was mine …

SON:

Ya well, it's not yours!
This is my place!

MANEEN: *[escalation of aggression]*

Your place!
Do ya hear that, Dad!?

[To Son] What makes you think this is your place!

SON: *[confused by question - unsure]*

It eh? It is my place?
It's always been my place!
I'm the oldest …

MANEEN:

The oldest?
The oldest what?

SON:

    Son.

MANEEN: [sarcastic]

    The oldest son?!
    Did it ever cross yer mind –
    when we were young fellas playin' cowboys and indians –
    Did ya ever stop and wonder –
    Why you were always Cochise!

SON: [confused]

    Cochise?

MANEEN:

    Cochise was a half-breed! Just like you!

SON: [Overlap – with above line]

    Ah, here we go again!

DADDA:

    Jesus Maneen!

[MANEEN and SON direct their argument via DADDA]

SON:

    The aul' half–brother lark, hah!?

MANEEN:

    Well it's true!
    And if he's gonna start pullin' rank – sayin' he's the oldest son,
    he'd want to know whose son he bloody well is!
    'Cause he's sure as fuck not yours!

DADDA:

    Back off now, Maneen! – I mightn't be his father –
    but I'm his Dad, and that's good enough for me!

SON:

If yer two son's turned out like him – this place would be well fucked!

MANEEN:

The oldest son, me hole!
You're a fuckin' half–breed

DADDA:

Jesus, Maneen!

SON:

You're an also–ran, Maneen!

MANEEN:

A what?

DADDA:

Shut up, Son!

SON: *[directly to DADDA]*

An also-ran!
That's what Dadda calls ya!
An also-ran!

MANEEN:

What's he fuckin' talkin' about!

DADDA:

Ah, well like I was only tryin' to exp …

SON:

This is all your fault!

DADDA: [DADDA *looks confused*]
>
> My fault?

[DADDA *is drawn into the spiralling argument – unable to get a word in he interjects into the escalating argument saying things such as : – Son! – Maneen! – Stop, Maneen!*
This scene ends in a frenzy of vitriol]

SON:

> All my life you've been takin' his side.
> Ever since we were young fellas.
> He didn't even as much as scratch his hole around this place.

MANEEN:

> Would ya listen to this!
> Come down offa' the cross, boy!
>
> [*Mocking/imitate*]
> All my life, you've been takin' his side …
> He's my father, and he's callin' you son! What more do ya want!

SON:

> The little big man himself hah?! Like lord of the manor.
> Put on the kettle, Son! Carry in me bags, Son!
> Get outa' me bed, Son! Give ya the night off, Son!
> Well I don't need no fuckin' night off from you!

MANEEN:

> Get over yerself boy!
>
> Since I was that height, I been listenin' to –
> the two of ye out here around the yard – as thick as thieves …
>
> I've every right to say what happens to this place!

SON:

> Just cause you've fucked up your own life
> doesn't mean ya can come back here year after year – fuckin'
> up ours!

MANEEN:

> Do ya know what's wrong with you!?
> Yer afraid!
> Yer afraid! Yer afraid ya might enjoy life!
> That's what's wrong with you!
> An' that's why ya rather be sittin' in the safety a' the car outside
> the bingo –
> or up talkin' to yer chickens …

[MANEEN makes chicken sounds Bak-bak! Bak-Bak!]

SON:

> Pissin' yer life away over in Dagenham!

MANEEN:

> … than be out in the real world –
> that's what wrong with you – Son!

SON:

> And my name is not Son!!

MANEEN:

> What do ya want to be called! Cochise? Brother?
> Or should that be half-brother? or half-fuckin'-breed!
> Or what ever the fuck you are –

DADDA:

> Cut it out, Maneen!

[DADDA attempts to intervene – but it spirals out of control]

SON:

> The big man in the long pants!
> [whisper] For fuck's sake!

DADDA:

> Son!

MANEEN:

> Happiest when you're up to yer neck in chicken shit!
> Bak-bak! Bak-Bak!

SON:

> Go back to yer Soho sluts!

DADDA:

> Son!

MANEEN:

> Martina Foley's only laughin' at you boy!

DADDA:

> Shut up, Maneen!

MANEEN:

> ... and yer presents of unfertilized eggs.
> For fuck's sake!

DADDA: [overlap]

> Maneen! Cut it out, Maneen! Right now!

MANEEN:

> Ya won't find me fingerin' through chicken shit lookin'
> for eggs – when I'm out lookin' for me hole!

SON:

>The big stud over in London –
>wanking yerself to death
>in yer kip of a bedsit!

DADDA:

>Son, shut up!

SON: *[to DADDA]*

>Maybe two wrongs don't make a right!
>But Jesus I've been wronged all my life,
>Are you gonna take his side again!

DADDA:

>I'm not takin' no one's side!

MANEEN: *[upset]*

>I'm the one who was squeezed out by the chosen one!

SON:

>Squeezed out!
>You got a wad a cash into yer hand when you fucked off to
>London!
>And you should fuck off back there again!

DADDA: *[Furious, reflecting earlier scene when SON and MANEEN were kids]*

>Will ye just cut it out the two a' ye! Jesus!
>It's the same every time!
>And I'm sick to fuckin' death of it!

SON:

>Yeah well he said ...

DADDA: *[continued fury]*

    I don't give a fuck who said what!
    It might look like he's the chosen one! [ref :SON]
    It might look like, me and Maneen have somethin' special.
    [ref: MANEEN]

    But that's not so –
    It's not so!
    It's just somethin' different that's all!

    Jesus Christ! I always treated ye different!

MANEEN: *[turns his anger on DADDA]*

    Yeah, well maybe ya should have treated us the same!

DADDA:

    Sur' Jesus, I treated ye different – 'cause ye are different!
    But I always treated ye different – in a an equal sorta' way!

MANEEN:

    Equal? I'm over in a bed sit in Dagenham –
    and he's here sitting on a chunk a' prime real estate!
    What the fuck is equal about that!

DADDA:

    That's the luck of the draw!
    This place was worth sweet shag-all when you left –
    and you were glad to go!

MANEEN:

    [hissed] Jeezus …

SON:

    And ya should shag off back to where you came from!

DADDA: *[absolutely furious – DADDA loses it]*
>Will ye shut the fuck up!
>Listen to me! Listen to me …
>The only thing in this world ye share is yer mother!
>I couldn't make head nor tail of her!
>She was always at war with herself
>And God knows the two of ye are the same!
>
>I was not able to save her from herself!
>And I sure as fuck can't save ye from each other!
>
>So whatever ye have to do –
>or say to each other!
>Ye can kill each other for all I care!
>Just leave me out of it!

[DADDA walks up stage]
[A moment or two of silence following crescendo of fury]

* * *

[A few days later – this most recent battle between SON and MANEEN is over – but is it a recurring cycle in their lives. It is a sibling rivalry fuelled by unresolved issues – issues that surface and erupt every time they encounter each other]
[In this scene the three characters speak directly to the audience they do not move and do not interact with each other except for maybe an odd cursory glance.]

DADDA: *[directly to audience]*
>Chalk and cheese …

SON: *[directly to audience - angry]*
>Always livin' in me small brother's shadow …
>But I'm not stepping back into the shadows for no one!

MANEEN:

Two types a' people in this world.
Them that works for money –
And them that makes money work for them …

DADDA:

A bit of a spark about Maneen.

SON:

Every time he comes home he drives me!

MANEEN: [directly to audience – angry/ disappointed]
Cork? Cork would do yer fuckin' head in …
Livin' in a time warp.
Had to get the fuck outa there …

SON:

He turns the whole place upside down and inside out – so he
do.
Even when we were young fellas!

DADDA:

Brains of a mechanic – hands of a surgeon.

MANEEN:

Ten years ago you couldn't give this place away …
But these days …

SON:

It's alwaysoolsomething else …
Have to wonder what's it gonna be next time …

DADDA:

Don't get me wrong,
I love me two boys.
But Jesus, when they get together, they're like a bag of cats …

* * *

[Son and Maneen – begin to move and react with one another – they have the appearance of chastened children. The atmosphere is wary, awkward but slightly conciliatory. Dadda continues to stay detached, maybe seated, and speaks directly to the audience.]

SON: *[to Maneen]*
> So?
> Y're headin' back, Maneen …

MANEEN:
> I am.

SON:
> Ya have all yer stuff packed?

MANEEN:
> I do.

SON:
> Sit in there I drop you up to the airport.

[Maneen reacts to the fact that Son is ordering him to sit into the car]

SON:
> Or, would you like to drive, Maneen?

MANEEN: *[still gets dig in about the clutch]*
> Naw, you can drive, Son.
> I might only be too heavy on the clutch.

DADDA: *[directly to audience]*
> Spends me whole life tryin' to keep 'em apart.
> But when two elephants go to war – 'tis the grass gets
> trampled.

SON:

>Throw in yer bags there so …
>You sure you have everything?

MANEEN:

>… sur' if I forgot anything,
>I'll be home again …

SON: *[alerts SON's sensitivities]*
>Home?!

[SON reacts visually]

MANEEN:

>Maybe Christmas time …

[SON reacts visually]

MANEEN:

>Or maybe before it!

DADDA: *[to audience]*
>Chalk and cheese?
>Chalk it down!

[SFX: Fade music]
[LX: Fade to black]

THE END.

BIOGRAPHY

Cónal Creedon is a novelist, playwright and documentary filmmaker. Appointed Adjunct Professor of Creative Writing at University College Cork in 2016.

Books

2018   Begotten Not Made – a novel published by Irishtown Press. Achieved recognition in NGBA Book Awards USA (2018), Readers Favourite Book Awards USA (2018), listed in selection of Best Books of the Year – Liveline RTÉ Radio 1, 'Book of The Year' – Irish Examiner (2018).

2017   Cornerstone – an anthology of student writing (editor). published by UCC and Cork City Libraries.

2015   The Immortal Deed of Michael O'Leary VC – published by Cork City Libraries.

2007   Second City Trilogy – a trilogy of internationally award winning stage plays, published by Irishtown Press. Commissioned by European Capital of Culture 2005. Productions in China, USA and Ireland.

1999   Passion Play – a novel cited as, Book of the Year [BBC Radio 4], Book of the Week [The Irish Examiner], Book on One [RTÉ 1 – Irish National Radio] and Book of the Week [RAI – Italian National Radio]. The novel has been translated into Italian, Bulgarian with extracts published in Germany, China.

1995   Pancho and Lefty Ride Out – a collection of short stories published by The Collins Press, Cónal's short stories have been published and broadcast extensively. His work has gained recognition in Life Extra Awards, Francis Mac Manus Awards, George A. Birmingham Awards, One-Voice Monologue Awards.

THEATRE

1999   When I Was God [Red Kettle Theatre Company]

2000   The Trial Of Jesus [Corcadorca Theatre Company]
Featured in National Millennium Celebrations.
Awarded two National Business to Arts Awards.
Nominated for Irish Times Theatre Awards.

2001   Glory be to the Father [Red Kettle Theatre Company]

2003   When I Was God. Blood In The Alley. Madder Market Theatre. UK

2005   The Cure [Cork Opera House / Blood in the Alley Theatre Co.]

2005   After Luke [Cork Opera House / Blood in the Alley Theatre Co.]

2005   The Second City Trilogy commissioned by European Capital of Culture.

2008   When I Was God – USA Premiere [Green Room Productions New York.]

2009   When I Was God & After Luke. [Irish Repertory Theatre New York]
Awarded Best Director. 1st Irish Theatre Awards New York
Nominated Best Actor. 1st Irish Theatre Awards New York.
Nominated Best Production. 1st Irish Theatre Awards New York.

2010   After Luke & When I Was God – Chinese Premiere, Shanghai World Expo.

2011   The Cure – JUE International Arts Festival, Shanghai, China.

2013   The Cure – USA Premiere. Green Room Theatre New York
Awarded Best Actor. 1st Irish Theatre Awards New York.
Nominated Best Playwright. 1st Irish Theatre Awards New York.

2014   When I Was God.
Fletcher Camross Drama Group. ICI Federation Drama Festival.
Awarded Best Actor. ICI Federation Drama Festival.
Awarded Best Supporting Actor. ICI Federation Drama Festival.

2016   The Cure – Showcase production, Irish Arts Centre Queens, New York.

2019   The Cure – Pigeon Productions. Arlene's Grocery, New York

Radio Drama

Cónal has penned over 60 hours of original fiction, short stories and plays, for radio. His work has represented Ireland in the World Play International Radio Drama Festival 2000 and has been broadcast on BBC Radio 4, BBC World Service, RTÉ.

1993   Come Out Now Hacker Hanley! [RTÉ radio 1]

1994   After the Ball. [Francis MacManus Awards]

1994   Every Picture tells a story. [RTÉ radio 1]

1994   Caught in a trap. [C.L.R Drama Competition-RTÉ]

1994–98 Under the Goldie Fish. [85 half hour episodes] [RTÉ Radio]

2000   This Old Man, He Played One. [World Play 3 International Festival]

2001   1601 [docu-drama Battle of Kinsale RTÉ]

2002   The Cure [Monologue-RTÉ]

2003   The Prodigal Maneen. [Awarded the C of I Bursary – RTÉ]

2003   Adaptation – Guests of the Nation [For Frank O' Connor Cent. – RTÉ]

2003   1601 – The March of O' Sullivan Beara. [RTÉ docu-Drama]

2004   Adaptation – Tailor and Ansty. [RTÉ Drama]

2004   Passion Play – Book on One. [RTÉ Radio 1]

2005   Adventure of the Downtown Dirty Faces. [5 short stories –
        RTÉ Radio 1]

2005   No.1, Devonshire Street. [BBC Radio 4]

TV Documentary/Film

2010   Flynnie, The Man Who Walked Like Shakespeare.[Producer/
        writer/director]
        Nominated Focal Documentary Awards. London UK.

2007   The Boys Of Fairhill. [Producer/writer/director]

2006   If It's Spiced Beef. [Producer/writer/director]

2006   Why The Guns Remained Silent In Rebel Cork. [Writer/
        director]

2005   The Burning of Cork. [Writer/director]

2001   A Man Of Few Words. [Short film produced by Indie Films]

1995   The Changing Faces Of Ireland. RTÉ [co-scripted six-part
        series]

Reading Tours include

Italy   4 city Reading tour Italy – 2001.
           Rome, Florence, Venice, Perugia.

UK.   Various reading tours.
           Dylan Thomas Centre – Swansea. 2000.
           Filthy McNasty's – London. 2001.
           Madder Market Theatre – 3 Cities Festival – Norwich. 2002.

USA.   Irish American Cultural Institute, 7 city coast-to-coast
           reading tour USA. 2007.
           New York, Albany, Rochester, Omaha, Montana, San
           Francisco, New Jersey.

China   Presented a number of reading tours to Shanghai, China.
           Shanghai International Literary Festival. 2008.
           Fudan Uni. Shanghai, People's Uni. Shanghai, Le Ceile
           Shanghai. 2009.
           Shanghai World Expo. 2010.
           Shanghai Jue International Arts Festival. 2010.
           M on the Bund & Shanghai Writer's Association. 2013.
           Guest of Honour – 10th Anniversary - Shanghai Writers'
           Association. 2017.

Austria   Sprachsalz Literary Festival. Tyrol Austria. 2014.

Germany   Launch of Cork Europa Erlesen – Translated by Jurgen
           Schnieder. Berlin. 2016.

Ireland.   Numerous readings at literary festivals.- Including,
           Keynote Speaker at Daniel Corkery Summer School. 2019.
           Speaker at Merriman Summer School. 2014.

www.ingramcontent.com/pod-product-compliance
Lightning Source LLC
Chambersburg PA
CBHW022153170626
46807CB00005B/2186